Date with Evil

Written By
Kevin Priestley

Order this book online at www.trafford.com
or email orders@trafford.com

Most Trafford titles are also available at major online book retailers.

Printed in Victoria, BC, Canada.

ISBN: 978-1-4269-3253-3 (sc)
ISBN: 978-1-4269-3254-0 (hc)
ISBN: 978-1-4269-3255-7 (eb)

Library of Congress Control Number: 2010906680

Our mission is to efficiently provide the world's finest, most comprehensive book publishing service, enabling every author to experience success. To find out how to publish your book, your way, and have it available worldwide, visit us online at www.trafford.com

Trafford rev. 05/27/2010

www.trafford.com

North America & international
toll-free: 1 888 232 4444 (USA & Canada)
phone: 250 383 6864 • fax: 812 355 4082

In memory of
Robert L. Priestley.
We love you.

"You may see them by night,
when the moon beams full over the valley,
which shall smell of death!"

Chapter 1

IF YOU GO DEEP into the heart of Georgia, you find a city by the name of Trench. Trench appears more as a small country town than a city living. Folks here are spread out, not close together as a county trailer yard. Its enough to be comfortable, though not so far spread that you could start your own farm. If you were to visit the city, you might notice that it has merely one grocery store, and only two stoplights. It's possible that the limited amount of businesses makes Trench appear smaller than it actually is. Throughout the city is a widespread of trees along with the occasional open field. The sun has falling to the horizon as dusk is upon the city. The sky is clear, a slight wind rustles bunches of leaves across the ground. The house of the Lastings family sets on top of a hill of lush green grass. A stone walk stretches across the yard and a mini van is parked in the drive. The house is that of two stories with hunter green curtains hanging in the window. A porch stretches out from the front extending the length of the house.

Derek Lastings is a tall man with sandy blond hair, good looking, and has intriguing blue eyes. He has recently reached the age of forty-two. His family consists of his wife Jennifer, whom is just two years younger than him and three children. Josie, the only girl, presently is seventeen years old, second oldest to her brother Michael of twenty-one years. Brad is their youngest child at four years old, a hyper young boy who often finds it hard to get along with others. Derek sits on the couch with his attention focused on the television set. Off in the dining room, Brad has pulled a stool over to the fish tank. The boy gives a small giggle as he opens the lid and begins repeatedly tapping on the inside of the glass. With in seconds every fish in the tank swarms to the top expecting dinner. The kid finds this very amusing. He stops momentarily to once again let them settle, then returns to rapping on the glass as he teases the poor creatures. Jennifer Lastings pulls some spices from the cupboard preparing to put the finishing touches on dinner. Michael would be joining them tonight mostly to visit. But she always would make more than enough just in case he would come hungry. Michael holds residence just outside of Trench, still only minutes from his parents.

The door swings open, Josie and her friend Lisa Mays walk in each holding bags of their own. Josie is rather tall for a girl, with brown hair that extends to her shoulders. The young girl has a very pretty face and a well-rounded body. Her green eyes dance when she's exited, as she is now. Lisa Mays is a little shorter than Josie with jet-black hair and brown eyes. She too has blossomed rather well. Both girls seem to be very lady like and brought up well. The two girls have been shopping since school had let out hours before. The dance would be the next night and both had to have the perfect dress for the occasion. Josie has a big smile on her face. She shuts the door behind her and places her bag in the chair just opposite of where Derek is sitting. From within the bag, Josie removes a pearl white dress apparently meant for her. It has spaghetti straps made from lace and looks to be extremely low cut.

"Dad, do you like my dress, it's for the school dance tomorrow? It's going to be so much fun." Josie exclaims.

Derek examines the piece before him, a disgruntled look comes over his face. "Well, why don't you go put it on and I will give you my opinion then, O.K.?"

Josie agrees then turns to the stairs, her friend waves as she goes by to be polite. The two climb the stairs and enter the door on the right. This is Josie's bedroom, your typical teenage living area. Posters of hot guys and favorite singers line each of the walls; an ancient ruins calendar sits on the girl's bed. Josie keeps many interests and always seems to be changing her mind. The two girls find their own corner of the room and begin to shed clothing. Moments later they both turn around to see how the other looks in her new dress. Lisa's cuts off about two inches above the knee and is a bright red. The shoulder straps were wider than that of Josie's dress, but both were a v-cut and very revealing. The white dress stops right at the knees. Both females look extremely beautiful. After prepping for a bit and telling one another how great each looks, the girls head back downstairs to show off.

Outside of Trench city limits, Michael Lastings pulls the door shut behind him as he exits his small one bedroom house. It's a little banged up, though it is plenty for a young adult living alone. Michael is a tall young man like his father and his hair is dark brown and long. He has a strong build and is a little scruffy in the face. His car is an old Ford Mustang around the year of eighty-four or five. Michael jumps in the car and turns over the engine. The car then pulls out of the driveway and squeaks a tire on the way out. Soon the boy would cross the city limits and from their it is just a few minutes to his mother and fathers. The road is narrow with trees on either side, Michael seems very relaxed with this. He drives these roads most every day and has become accustomed to the lack of pavement. The sun is steadily dropping in the sky and night is quickly moving in. Michael flips his lights on to see just a little better, then speeds further along. With out any warning at all, something appears in the road ahead. The car heads straight for it. Startled, the young man stomps the brake with both feet. The small car screams to a stop just before hitting the thing before him.

As Michael looks up from the steering wheel he becomes very uneasy at the sight in front of him. Before him stands a black wolf, back arched and fangs gleaming in the headlights. His breath becomes trapped in his lungs as he is frozen with fear. Fortunately the beast eases away, then scampers back within the forest. Michael releases a great breath of air and gathers himself. He pauses a few moments longer before accelerating again. The rest of the way to his parents, Michael takes it slowly and cautiously.

Just down the street from the Lastings live Mr. and Mrs. Larry Bora. Currently the two are finishing up a little yard work as daylight slips away. They are two elder folks, lived all their lives in the city of Trench. Larry Bora is short and stocky, still with a full head of hair, gray of course, not bad for a man in his seventies. His wife Delores has lost most of her hair and has become slightly over weight. The two live just three houses from the Lastings and both households are rather fond of the other. The Bora's look up to the sound of a horn and wave as Michael drives by. They look on as the young adult parks his vehicle and then enters the house. His mother greets him immediately with a hug and a kiss on the cheek.

"I fixed extra just in case you were hungry," Jennifer exclaims as she enters the dining room. Jennifer, not looking a day over thirty, has hazel eyes, and long black hair that reaches her shapely behind. The woman smiles warmly and urges her son for a hug.

"Thanks mom, I am famished," Michael replies as he embraces his mother. Josie and Lisa look on still wearing their new dresses. Michael acknowledges them both.

"Wow, you two look incredible, I heard about the dance tomorrow night."

Josie looks to her mom and laughs, "Gee, I don't know who could have told you about it."

Jennifer smiles and returns to the kitchen, the two girls run upstairs to change for dinner. Michael and his father Derek exchange a handshake, as he begins to tell him of his eerie encounter on the way over.

Meanwhile, two fishermen pull their reels from the lake to rebate the hooks. A fire a few feet away illuminates a large part of the area around them. Mark Salem is one of the fellows; his hair is scraggly and blond but short. He is the age of about thirty and looks to be a little overweight. Along with him is his good friend Eugene Browder, maybe a little younger, though he seems to have similar lifestyles.

This man has black curly hair to match his full beard and mustache. Eugene is near the same size of his friend; both men probably could stand to lose forty to fifty pounds. Mark takes his line in hand and slides a worm right over the hook. Then he prepares to cast back out. The two men let their lines stream out a bit then drop in the water before them.

"I'm gonna catch me a whopper, like one you have never caught," Mark brags as he sets his pole neatly resting against a y shaped stick. Eugene says nothing, only shakes his head. Moments go by as the two fishermen await an unsuspecting fish to be lured in. Then Eugene hollers, "I got one! I got one!"

The man lifts his fishing pole into the air giving a slight jerk to assure whatever is biting becomes hooked. Beginning to reel the seemingly large fish in, both men become startled by a noise just down the bank. Mark is the first to find where the noise came from, he stands straight up and then stumbles back. Eugene slowly turns just to drop his pole at the sight of what stands before them. Only yards away is a beautiful but dangerous all black wolf, again the beast snarls and arches it's back. Quickly Mark begins to dig amongst his tackle box pulling a knife from within. Both men stand their ground terrified at the thoughts running through each ones mind. The wolf stares, the glare of the fire burning in its blue eyes. What happens next completely shocks the two friends. The animal turns to the water, its teeth gleaming in the moonlight and releases a great howl. From its open jaws springs a black flying shadow, at a closer look the shadow becomes that of a bat, which disappears into the night. The wolf then loses all life and collapses, vaporizing into the ground below. Mark and Eugene look on with mixed emotions of surprise and horror. They turn and look at one another then cautiously walk toward the area in which the beast once stood. The closer they became to this spot, the more obvious it becomes that now nothing remains.

Eugene tries to speak, but no words will come out. Mark stutters still in amazement.

"I, I do not believe, I do not believe what just happened."

Mark could do little more than shake his head in agreement, and though nothing is said, both men give the other the impression. "Lets get the hell out of here." Soon all the supplies is packed except for Eugene's fishing pole, which the tide along with the fish on the other end has pulled into the lake. Leaving the fire burning, the men take off with tales between their legs. The fire is no concern at this point, nor is the loss of a fishing rod. Of course after seeing what they had, not much would be of any concern.

Chapter 2

THE LASTINGS FAMILY HAVE just finished up their dinner.

For the moment they remain sitting at the table conversing. Only Brad has food left in front of him, he continues to play with it as if the food were some kind of toy or something. Jennifer tries her best but the boy still refuses to eat. Josie's friend Lisa has left only minutes ago, though she did not eat with them due to other plans. Her boyfriend Tommy Critton intends to serve the girl a late night dinner and a movie. Lisa's parents would not mind too much, they got along well with the boy. The evening grows short and soon Michael decides it time to turn homeward. By this time the boy has all but forgotten his earlier run in with the wolf. As for Josie, she would watch television for a bit before going to bed. As for Mr. and Mrs. Lastings, they were left to fight with Brad. Every night has become a choir just getting the kid to get in bed. Finally, upon midnight, all has turned quiet and the Lastings now sleep peacefully.

Lisa and Tommy are finishing up at the restaurant they had chose to eat at. Tommy gathers the trash in one spot on the table and leaves a few bucks for a tip. Lisa pushes her chair in as her boyfriend begins to wrap her jacket around her. On the way out a passing manager thanks them for the service, the two smile then continue outside. The couple has already been to a movie prior to eating dinner. Typical teenagers, eating popcorn before they have even eating dinner. Almost to the car, Lisa becomes startled as three men step from within the shadows. Tommy recognizes the crew entirely too much. Its Lisa's ex-boyfriend and his goons for friends. His name is Larry Stant, and his buddies are none other than Kevin Riley and Barry Spencer. These guys are a bunch of no gooders at school and did not tend to like Tommy very much. Tommy had been through many unpleasant run ins with the group. With no intention of any trouble, Critton follows his girl to the passenger side of the vehicle, pops the round key into the lock and unlocks and opens her door for her.

"Well isn't that sweet, he's getting the door for her. Come on guys, isn't it sweet?" Barry and Kevin laugh at Stant's comments. Tommy rolls his eyes then walks back to the driver side of his car preparing to enter it and quickly leave a bad situation. Larry Stant moves in closer, the two guys behind him keep a close distance. The boys look and dress just like your ordinary high school troublemakers. Before Tommy can reach his side, Larry steps into his path blocking the way between him and his car door.

"Looks like you and my girl are having a good time, unfortunately for you, I don't like it when my girl enjoys herself with another guy," he utters.

Tommy bites his lip and retaliates, "Well, she is no longer your girl Larry, you need to get over it man. Listen, I don't want trouble from you and your boys here. So if you will, just let me by."

Barry Spencer chimes in, talking like some sort of wigger with an attitude. "Yo man, we mean no trouble fool, Just funning with you. Maybe trying to get a rise out of you or something. And another thing, if we were here for trouble, you would have known it by now. Shit!"

Tommy cautiously brushes by the obstacle before him and slowly opens his car door. Larry and the others continue to glare at him, never taking their eyes off himself and Lisa. With a small sigh of relief, Tommy pulls his car door shut. Now he starts the engine and takes off, putting as much distance between Larry Stant and Lisa as quickly as possible. The couple is silent most of the way home, Lisa silently thinks about what has occurred, and hopes the guy beside her is not too upset over it.

"I'm sorry he has to be that way, please do not be upset with me Tommy," she says pleadingly.

Right off, Critton says nothing at all, only drives on searching for some response inside his head. Then the boy lets out a small grin, "It is all right. I am kind of getting used to his childish little games. Besides, it is not your fault Larry Stant is obsessed with you, its just your incredible good looks along with those sexy legs." Lisa lights up with a smile and grabs Tommy's hand knowing all is going to be fine. Upon arrival to the girls house, he again very gentleman like gets Lisa's door for her. The lovebirds now say their good nights and Lisa heads on inside to bed. Tommy gets back in his car then slowly leaves his girl friends street. Having done so, the boy reaches over and pushes a tape into his radio. As the beat of rock and roll enters the air, his volume is turned up considerably. Next the young man finds his own way home, for this night has now come to an end.

Chapter 3

As the sun rises in the sky, it gives birth to a new day. The ocean surrounds a small forgotten island a few miles off shore. Waves shatter upon the jagged terrain as if it were glass dropping upon the rocks. A large rock formation sits along this body of land filled with caves and crevices. The wind carries in a familiar flying shape, as the object arrives closer to the island we can see it is the black bat from earlier. Suddenly the mysterious flying creature flutters, then streams into a long black cloak. The wind catches it a bit, though it still comes to rest on the ground below. Moments later, something stirs from beneath the cape, it rises up from beneath the cloth and slowly takes the form of man. We can only see the eyes of this character as the cloak is covering all other features. Its eyes are dark and eerie looking. Now as man, the thing disappears into one of the many crevices before him. Inside the cold rock it is very dark and somewhat damp from the moisture of the water. Small dust particles shoot through the air as wind brushes into the cave. The man, or creature, creeps further along the narrow depths of the stonewalls until he comes to a dim lit corridor. Spiders and many other species of insect scatter upon his arrival, a lone lamp sets on a square like rock only feet away. Many cobwebs dangle from the ceiling and small cracks curse the floor below. From the midst of the darkness above climbs another being. All black covers his body. He gingerly reaches the floor then slowly turns to see who has come before him. Hundreds of years of age plague the old man, his long gray hair reaches the back of his knees. A skinny wrinkled face shows solemnly in the lowly light from the lamp. The old man's eyes have sank back away form his eye sockets, no color remains only blackness. A long blood red cape extends down the aged being's back and trials behind him. At this point he seems to be little more than a skeleton with skin and remaining hair. The dark creature looks feeble and powerless, but a light aura around him shows the complete strength of his powers. We now return to a younger, more completely covered being as he speaks.

"Father, I have found little to show me the way to the rare blood type that you have requested. It is as if the substance does not exist, even though I certainly know other wise."

"I have asked you to call me Abraham my son, but that is not the issue at this very precise moment. As for the rare blood, it is for my very life that I have need for it, for the ability to live on. You must look deep within, taste what it is that I have sent you for. It is there, and you must find it. Now, this is the only way to live on for all of us, now go, your brothers Ash and Ambrose will soon be along with you. I wish I could go myself, but although I am strong with power here, I would be weak as a child outside of this realm. Never mind all that, between you three, I know I shall have what it is I need."

Abraham's son lets him complete his words, and then he turns back to the ocean. The wind blows with great gusts. The being stands solid before it, then any trace of man disappears beneath the ever present cloak. Once again the black bat comes and the wind quickly whisks it away.

Elsewhere, the Lastings family all lay still asleep in their beds. An alarm clock on Derek's dresser reads the present time as Eight-

Thirty. In the distance we hear the sound of a phone ringing to life, Derek quickly awakes and moves slowly from within his warm bed. He does his best to get to the phone before it awakes the rest of the household. "Hello!"

Lastings boss Daryl Form tones up on the other end, "Yes um, is this Derek?" Great, listen um, we have a little bit of a going on down here. I hate to wake you on your usual day off, but do you think you could come on down and give us a hand."

Reluctantly. "Well, I guess I could come on and help for a little while, as long as I am off in time to see my daughter off to her dance." Derek pauses for a moment then fires the question. "So what is going on?"

"Little bit of a paint spill, nothing spectacular though!"

As the phone conversation comes to an end, Derek carefully hangs up the phone and rolls his eyes as doing so. Now he would get his clothes together and be on his way. Mixing paints hardly seemed to be the boy hood dream Lastings remembered, but hell, it paid the bills. Normally today and Sunday would be his day off, of course every job has it's exceptions. He thinks once more about his daughters dance that night and again hopes he will be home in time to see her off. Once fixing a quick breakfast and, if you will, wolfing it down, the man runs off to work. Jennifer Lastings begins to stir in her lonely bed; she rarely sleeps with out the presence of her husband. With sleepy eyes and an exhausted look on her face, Jennifer makes her usual early morning trip to the bathroom. While on the john, she begins to think about what she can get done. Grocery shopping seemed the best answer; this way the amount of people shopping would be at a medium. After a hot shower and a quick phone call, Jennifer readies herself for her errand. She always goes shopping with an old friend from high school. The friend would pick her up in a small mini-van and the two ladies would go their own way.

Upstairs, an alarm clock blares on as it bears the time of nine-thirty. Josie Lastings rests for a time, then reaches over and pats at the off button. The girl never did have any use for a snooze button, unlike the rest of the world. The young lady decides to get up, this would give her an hour and a half before needing to be at work. Josie is only seventeen, yes, but does not mind working weekends for a little extra cash. Currently she works as a server at a local restaurant a couple miles out of Trench. Today she would work an eleven to six shift, which would give her plenty of time to ready her self for the dance later. So she gathers some things then runs down stairs still wearing her nightgown. She looks on as her little brother Brad fights with Jennifer as the woman continues the task of readying the boy to go out. Josie follows the hall way to the linen closet and grabs a towel. The girl then turns down the longer hallway and enters the bathroom. Locking the door behind her she sets her things down on the side of the sink. Upon removing her nightgown, the girl reveals her hourglass shape of a body. Josie then peers into the mirror, lifting her tits slightly she pronounces. "Not bad, not too bad at all." Eventually she readies the water then steps into the shower.

The sound of a horn rings out from the street; Jennifer peers out the window finding a familiar van parked out front. Quickly she picks up the now ready Brad and walks out the door. A note on the table reads to Josie,

Hi love,

Off to the grocery store, wont be to long. Please be careful on your way to work and don't work to hard. Love,

Mom

Now in the car, the three as a group head for the city grocery store. Bradford does his best to annoy Jennifer's friend; only, its to no avail.

As Jennifer Lastings does her grocery shopping, her son Michael, along with a group of friends, reach the basketball court. This indeed is Michael's favorite sport; he often gets some friends together for a good time. First they play a couple games of twenty-one, then the group turns to three on three. Michael and his five friends play on for hours. Naturally they occasionally stop for a drink and a quick breather, though for the most part they just play on. Game after game go by until the guys are too exhausted to play anymore. One of Michael's buddies, Steven Mass call out.

"Who is for lunch and drinks at Caroline's?"

This restaurant he speaks of is where Josie works, Michael likes the idea of visiting his sister and the others agree as well. Steven, who has been Michael's pal the longest, rides with him. As young Lastings strolls over to the cars with the other young men, a strange figure stands before them. The young man appears to be in his mid twenties. A black cloak covers the man along with that of a blood red cape. He bears dark looking eyes, dirty blond hair, and a mustache on his face. The group looks on in awe as the being speaks.

"You may seem them by night, when the moon beams full over the valley, which shall smell of death!"

The boys all look at each other not knowing exactly what to do. The man before them seems to stare a hole right through each and every one of them. Slowly they all decide to pile into their vehicles, the figure looks on with eyes as dark as night. Michael has become a little frightened; he tries not to let it show, no matter how difficult. The rest of his buddies seem to be at a loss themselves. When the vehicles pull away, a feeling of relief comes over all. Michael can not help but to take one last look as he pulls away. As he does, his feeling of relief turns to that of horror. The strange being stands there solemnly, and then lets out a great hiss, fangs protrude from his mouth. They look like the type you would see in an old scary movie. Michael shudders as he turns back to watching the road and attempts to ignore it all. Steven looks at him a little funny then turns his attention back to the courts, the mysterious man has gone! Mass asks young Lastings what he has seen, he shakes his head as if to say nothing. His friend knows better though.

Now we find Josie at Caroline's restaurant, the place appears very busy. An impatient customer calls for his check, another complains about the food taking to long. The young lady keeps her cool, never missing a beat. Her busy day trudges on and the rude customers come and go. Finally the rush comes to an end, Josie leaves her last customers with the check then goes to the back for a break between tables. She sits on a wooden stool awaiting the next bunch of jerks to test her patience. She begins to think about that nights dance; a long black limousine would pull up in front of the school. Two good-looking young fellows would exit the vehicle and let the two girls out. Her and Lisa would step form the vehicle then proceed into the dance. Tommy would then take Lisa's side escorting the ladies up the front stairs. Two brilliantly good-looking men open either door to allow the three to enter. Craig Johnson would then walk up smiling and staring at Ms. Josie Lastings. She puts out her hand, he gladly grasps it then lays a kiss on the back of it. To her, Craig Johnson is the best looking guy in Trench High school, and he happens to be an incredible athlete. Josie has had a crush on him for some time now, perhaps why she does not have a date for the big dance. Now Josie and Craig walk arm and arm onto the dance floor. Her favorite slow song begins to play, the couple moves closer together. Johnson begins to kiss the young lady as his hands run smoothly over her shapely body. He starts down her neck, almost nibbling on it and she suddenly feels very warm. Only the two of them are there now, Craig lifts her dress up then slides his powerful hand down into her panties. Josie groans in anticipation of what is to come. The dance is gone. All that exists in the world is she and her man. The music has faded to almost nonexistent, the strobe lights no longer flash across the walls. Now, it is just her and Craig!

Chapter 4

"Josie, hey Josie, are you O.K.?" Fellow employee Susan Falls calls.

Josie snaps out of it looking all hot and bothered. "Huh, Oh! Yeah I'm fine. Just, um, Just day dreaming a little Susan, what do you need?"

The woman replies, "You have a table dear. Your brother and a few of his friends are here and of course they want you as their server. I just sat them in your section."

"O.K.," Josie agrees. She stands up and checks herself in a nearby mirror, then prepares to return to work. Next she finds her way out to the table in which Susan has sat for her. Michael and five of his friends sit before her. She recognizes a couple of them, like Steven Mass and a couple that worked with her brother. Kenny Marks, Dale Sanders, and Timothy Smilot. The other one she really is not sure, Mike, as she would sometimes call her brother, introduces everyone. The six of them are all drenched in sweat and look undoubtedly thirsty. So she takes all the orders, quickly gets them drinks, and then puts in food orders. Timothy Smilot lifts his soda to drink, moments later he sits it back down on the polished wooden table.

"Guys, at the ball court, whoever that man was certainly gave me a bad feeling. I mean, what in the world could that have meant? Moonlight on the valley and the smell of ... Death!" Timmy seems reluctant to talk over this matter, only her has to know how the others feel. Steven Mass speaks up.

"It was a little freaky the way his eyes were all dark, and the outfit he had on was like something of Gothic nature. Man, I am just glad to be away from that strange character!" Michael opens his mouth to speak then decides against it. Dale Sanders chimes in.

"It was just some stupid joke guys. I mean you all were not really afraid of that guy were you? I would hate to think I am hanging out with a bunch of pussies!" Dale always tries to act like the tough guy, its his nature.

"Shut up!" Michael calls sharply. I myself think we were all a little frightened, and that includes you Dale. Listen, I seen something as we were driving off. That thing had fangs, and I mean dagger like fangs. It scar..."

"Is that what made you jump," Steven asks interrupting. This was one of his few character flaws, that and belching. But hey don't we all have a flaw here and there. "I knew something was going on, but you told me nothing. I should have known better, and I did."

"Oh come on y'all, we sound ridiculous. Fangs, valley, death? Can't you see we are being played for fools here? He was just trying to get us worked up and apparently he did a fine job. I mean come on," pleads Dale Sanders.

Before anyone can make a comeback, Josie arrives with everybody's plate. She sits each plate in its proper spot in front of each of them. Including the one she did not know. Hey, she is working for a tip here. Kenny Marks and Dale Sanders immediately begin to eat. The others kind of look at one another, maybe to see what would be said next. Or would the subject change. Michael pours a little bit of salt on his fries then shoves a couple into his mouth. The table has turned from almost heated words to complete quiet. Lastings decides to be the first to break the silence.

"Anyway guys, rather you believe me of don't, I know what it was that I seen. Regardless of the fact, I think we need to change the subject."

Dale Sanders finished chewing a bite of food. "Well, I have a subject, lets talk about how good your sister looks in those jeans."

"Hey, Hey!" Michael warns.

The rest of the group laughs as the two guys throw peanuts at one another. Then a hush comes over them as Josie returns to the table to bring them their check.

"And I quote," I hate to see her leave. But I sure love to watch her go." Kenny Marks has to make a joke himself to try and look cool in front of Dale. The two get along, although Kenny seems to be more of a tag along to Sanders than a friend.

Again every one laughs at the remark, except Michael of course. He only sits in his spot beginning to look flush. Finally the group lays the money for the meal and the server's tip on the table and leaves.

Derek Lastings eyes the clock on the wall, it reads a few minutes after four. The paint spill has almost been dealt with by now. Even though it was only a small paint spill, even the tiniest one can be a pain in the ass. Now, seven hours after Lastings had arrived, the floor is finally cleared. Once punching the time clock, Lastings leaves for home, anxious to see his daughter off to the dance. On the way out Derek crosses paths with Mark Salem. The man looks to be a little tired, maybe even a little crazed.

"Derek, hey how's the job, on my way in myself."

"Well", he began as he wipes sweat from his brow. "We just got finished with a spill containment, pretty rough too. What's going on with you, ya look a little tired?"

Salem inches a little closer and then takes a peak around. "I did not sleep very much good last night. Seen something the other day that would make a man think he was losing his mind. If Eugene had not seen the darn thing too, hell, I'd know I was crazy."

"What Mark, what do you think you have seen?"

"I have not told anyone cause, its a little insane." I'll tell you but just don't tell any one else."

A look of bewilderment appears on Derek Lastings face, "All right, O.K." Derek agrees.

"Well, Eugene and myself were doing some fishing at the old lake. I had my tackle there and my knife. When that thing changed I could not believe my own eyes. It was incredible, I mean it was amazing. Like nothing I've eve...

"What was incredible, your not making any sense man," Lastings states as he interrupts.

"Sorry Derek, there was this wolf, a black one. It showed it teeth and looked as if to attack. I grabbed my knife, but then, but then it just kinda, disappeared into a bat," Mark explains!

Derek does not look convinced, the man shakes his head then begins to walk on, with no intent of being rude, just does not know what to say. He takes a few steps then turns back to Mark.

"Your right, don't tell anyone, I sure wont."

As Derek grows farther away, Salem kind of glares in his own disgust. He knew no one would believe him, it was crazy. He had hopes Derek would have taking him just a little more serious. Continuing on Salem tries to forget about it.

Robert Falls clicks off the radio then proceeds to the kitchen for a snack. Him and Susan often kept lots of goodies in the house for times like these. Robert could remember the time they first met. They were both standing in line waiting to buy a ticket for 'Titanic', a candy bar of the same taste in their hands. The couple hit it right off, and has been together seven years. Now they own a single story three-bedroom house, with no kids. Its located merely a block from Caroline's restaurant, perfect for Susan. Robert opens the refrigerator and peers inside, nothing really suites his fancy though. A noise rattles in from the evening room, causing the man to bang his head on the refrigerator. Falls now looks curiously in the direction in which the noise came. An immensely large crash overtakes the front room. Robert stumbles back, partly from fright and partly just from unknowing what has entered his home. With great ease and caution, the man walks to the doorway. In the middle of his house stands a man he has never seen before, and he looks comfortable to be there as well. This is the same man that appeared as the boys were leaving the ball court. Naturally, Robert Falls does not know this, nor does it matter either way. A strong and eerie feeling crawls up Falls back. As the threat before him moves in, Susan's husband backs toward the kitchen once again. He fumbles to retrieve a weapon from the silverware drawer, it is of no use. The man is coming too fast.

"What do you want, "demands Robert as the figure keeps coming?

The dark being pauses for a moment then speaks. "I am Ambrose, you may have something we need! I am here to take it."

The sharpness in the man's voice stuns Robert Falls, he wonders what the man could have meant by we. Fortunately, the man would soon find out. Ambrose backs Robert to the opposite side of the kitchen. Then with in the blink of an eye the door behind him springs open. Falls spins around to meet his on comer, as he does a cold hand meets his throat. It feels almost as ice, and the grip is strong, incredibly strong. As the grip continues to tighten, Robert can do nothing. The breath begins to leave the helpless mans lungs. Now, Ambrose unsheathes a brilliant dagger from with in his black cloak. And with a quick slice, Falls collapses to the floor. His neck has been slit wide open, Ash who quite abruptly made his appearance, smiles at his brother Ambrose. The two could have been identical twins if not for the mustache in which Ambrose wears on his face. Ash, has no facial hair, only thick black eyelashes and hair to match. Both reveal knife like fangs hidden in their mouths. Blood stains the kitchen tile, a vein has been hit and the fluids continue to spew! Ambrose replaces his dagger in its sheath, then moves to a nearby cupboard. After taking a look inside, the unholy being removes a drinking glass the size of little more than a coffee cup. An expression of evil comes to the face of each of these Gothic creatures. Next the kitchen item becomes placed against Robert Falls' neck, forcing blood to squirt out and into the fragile glass. At three-quarters full, Ambrose pulls it away and raises the vile to the air. It glistens in the daylight that pours in a nearby window. The bright light seems to be no more a bother to them than it would to a normal human. Ambrose now pulls the cup to his lips and begins to drink. He leaves only a taste remaining. Ash quickly gulps it down then places it on the counter.

"Tasty", Ambrose begins, "but not what we are looking for." With this, the two vampires leave the scene as is. Robert Falls' body lies on the kitchen floor, his blood covering the new tiled floor. There's a glass with spots of blood setting on the counter, and a couple bloody footprints.

Chapter 5

BACK IN THE CITY of Trench, Josie Lastings gets ready for an evening of fun. It is about seven o'clock and the dance would be starting in just one hour's time. Lisa would be meeting her about seven-thirty and her parents could take both the girls to the dance. Josie can hardly keep her excitement inside. She remembers back to last years autumn dance. Her and Lisa had so much fun. Of course she was still with Tommy back then, and Josie went with John Bell, what a name that was. She always did hate it' but hell, the guy had been a hunk, so what's the big deal. Afterwards they all four went to the last showing of one of Bruce Willis' latest movies. It was the dance that most of the good times came though. All the good songs were played and the DJ had been extremely cool. Josie hoped this year would prove just as great as the year before. The girl opens her top drawer and removes a lacy bra from within, now she fastens it on, her thoughts still on the last dance. The pretty young woman walks to her closet, she takes her dress from the hanger and the special plastic that keeps it, and begins to slip it on. After fixing her hair and make-up, Josie proceeds down stairs. Her mother Jennifer meets her at the bottom step to tell her how beautiful she looks in her outfit. Across the room young Brad plays in the fish tank, poor creatures. Derek pulls himself away form the television and gets up off his comfortable couch to see how his little girl looks. Might I say she is a sight to see, and is not exactly his little girl any more.

Any moment, Lisa would be pulling up with her parents, Josie gives her father a kiss then gathers her coat and purse. Brad runs in from the fish tank wanting a hug from sissy. His hands are quite wet and do not need to get on his sisters lovely dress.

"Mama, put me down, down, down!" Brad begins to scream at the top of his lungs.

"Now you hush, c'mon we are going to dry those hands off, then you can give Josie a hug. Not only that, if you did not play in the fish tank we would not have this problem."

Derek eyes his daughter with a bit of unease. He tries not to let it show too much. "So, what time should old dad expect you home," asks Mr. Lastings.

Josie grins, "Well, two-o'clock sounds good to me, please!"

"Oh you're killing me Josie. I guess its O.K., go on and have some fun," Derek exclaims trying to hide his worries.

"Thanks dad, I love you." Josie gives her dad a kiss on the cheek followed by a hug. Two a.m. is two more hours than he would usually give, so the young girl knew her dad was being easy to get along with. A knock on the door interrupts the father daughter moment. Derek opens the door, "C'mon in, we would like to get a few pictures of the girls."

Lisa's parents chime in, "That's a great idea."

Josie and her best friend go over to the fireplace and stand side by side. The camera flashes and they are asked to pose for another one. Lisa has gotten accustomed to getting her picture taking, Josie's parents always seem to have film around the house. The camera flashes a couple more times, then the girls anxiously make their way to the door.

"Have fun you two, Jennifer begins. Your gonna need a stick to keep the boys away!" All laugh at mom's silly comments. Josie gives her parents a hug and a kiss then heads out the door. Lisa's parent's follow and the four pile into the family car. The girls pretty much gossip the whole way to the dance. "Did you hear that..." and "Did you know..," typical teenage girls. Then Josie begins to talk about how great Craig Johnson is and Lisa brags about Tommy, who would be meeting them at the dance by the way. The vehicle comes to a rest at one of the few city stoplights and a black Chevrolet Blazer pulls up along side them.

"Man Lisa, look at that hunk sitting in the truck next to us, I mean he is no Craig or Tommy, but he is looking all right. Definitely nothing wrong about that!"

Lisa glances over to take in the view that Josie is so involved in. Behind the wheel of the Blazer is a man dressed in a pure black tuxedo and coat. A dark red tie hangs around his neck as he relaxes in his seat. The man is still of a young age, clean shaving and has dark green eyes. of course the girls cannot see them in the dark.

"He looks a little strange to me, gives me the creeps. I mean there just is not enough color, black and dark red," Lisa exclaims apprehensively.

As the light turns green, Josie says. "Well, I kind of like the cold and dark kind. I think mysterious is so handsome and interesting."

Lisa laughs and shakes her head, both girls stare as the Chevrolet Blazer flies by the slower moving sedan. They are almost to the dance, a feeling of anxiousness comes over both young ladies. Lisa can hardly wait to see her Tommy in his tuxedo, he will look so good. Josie Lastings thinks about how many guys she will dazzle and make them wish they had come stag themselves. Finally after what seems like an eternity, the girls arrive at the dance. Both of their faces light up with a beautiful smile. Lisa's father exits the vehicle and opens the door for both Josie and Lisa. Lastings thinks back to her daydream at work momentarily then steps out of the vehicle. Both smile at the scene before them, the father hugs his daughter and acknowledges Josie then turns and leaves. The High school steps stand in front of them. At the top, draped from the roof above hang long and brightly colorful streamers. An incredibly large banner stretches across the entire front of the school. In extra large letters is written, "Welcome to the Trench High School Autumn dance!" Lisa looks in awe as the letters across the front of her school seem to be larger than her. The ladies move slowly up the steps taking notice of every little decoration along the way. The doors stand before them now, mirror like wrapping paper cover each separate entrance. The school has never looked so good to the two young women. The heads of the dance committee did a wonderful job. Two men, dressed in expensive suits, stand at either side of the way in, they proceed to open the doors. The two radiant and beautiful girls look at each other in almost an ecstatic state. Josie Lastings and Lisa Mays get like this every year, hardly able to contain themselves. Now, all at once the two girls walk in to the dance smiling ear to ear!

Chapter 6

THE FULL MOON SHOWS bright in the sky, trees outline a wide valley off the edge of Trench city limits. Three men stand alone in the shadows, the smell of death plagues the air. They all dress in the same attire, all black with blood red cloaks around them. Darkness makes it too difficult to see their faces. They begin to walk the distance of the long bearing valley. Every full moon comes another meeting just as this one. The wind picks up a bit and then comes a howl that is heard for miles around. The end of the valley draws near and the three nocturnal beasts draw to their hands and knees. The form of man slowly vanishes, and that of wolves are all that remains. They are the colors of black, gray, and white. Looking wildly around the animals snarl and again let out a howl. This one seems much lower than the first, but still powerful. Then, quickly the three scurry off into the depths of the trees around them.

Back at Trench City High School, the music booms from within and strobe lights flash all around. The gymnasium has now been filled with students and everyone looks to be having a great time. Craig Johnson, Josie's personal crush, wows a couple girls with his ingenious dance maneuvers. Kevin Riley, Barry Spencer and Larry Stant stand conversing off in a corner by themselves. Tommy Critton waits at a table for his girl to arrive. Josie and Lisa soon enter the gym, the music becomes overwhelming. A couple of fellow students whistle at the two dolls as they strut by. Lisa walks anxiously to the reserved table at the opposite side of the gym. Josie does her best to keep up with her friend, while doing so she admires the decorative autumn leaves spread over the walls. Meeting the girls half way, Tommy embraces Lisa with both arms. He wears a completely white tuxedo with a sassy tie and cummerbund.

"Wow you look delicious, sometime later I will have to see if you taste as sweet as you look," Tommy says intensively.

"You look damn good yourself, and uh, watch the comments around friends all right." Lisa giggles a little and kisses her man on the cheek.

Josie steps back and admires the two of them together, "What a wonderful pair you two make, both like to flatter the other one."

Tommy laughs and teases Lisa as he replies, "You know, if Lisa was not here I would be chasing you around."

He receives a playful slap for his efforts and Josie smiles a thank you. Then, a couple yards away, Craig Johnson catches young Ms. Lastings eye. With out saying a word to the others she begins to walk his way. Two other girls presently stand with her hunk of a crush. Josie tries to make eye contact though it is to no avail. She moves a little closer and starts dancing to the music, more for him to notice than anything else. He eyes her for a moment then returns to flirting with either of the girls at his side. It s good to know her attempts do not go unnoticed as she begins to dance a little more.

"Hey where are you going girl, asks Lisa from behind.

Josie stops in her tracks and turns around. Lisa realizes what is happening right away. Craig had noticed her and for now, that was enough. Josie throws her arms up to act like she didn't know what she had been doing, then went back with the others to have some fun. The bass form the music seems to shake the walls, couples dance on enjoying every moment.

Yelling above the music, Lisa calls to Tommy and Josie, "Would you like to go for refreshments or is it a little too early in the game?"

"No it's not too early, sounds like a pretty good idea to me. How about you Josie?" She nods a yes and the group heads back up to the front of the gymnasium where the snacks and drinks are held. Up at the entrance, a small argument ensues. The young man Josie and Lisa had seen in the Chevrolet Blazer is trying to make his way in to the dance. A dark haired thin man stands in his way, he's one of the many teachers of Trench high.

"I told you, no one outside of Trench High School students are allowed in unless accompanied by one of our students," the teacher's words are firm and confident.

The young man speaks back, kind of monotone but seemingly with lots of patience. "A friend has already arrived here, she is waiting for me inside." The guy sounds pretty convincing but the man before him does not seem to be buying it.

"I'm sorry, there is just no way I can let you go in there, I'm only doing my job." A slight chill runs up the chaperone's back as the young man peers deep into his eyes. It feels almost as if some one has taking an icy cold finger and ran it up the length of his back.

"Well, I would hate to keep you from your job, I will just leave then. Wait, I see her now. Hey, Josie!"

The young man calls to Lastings as if he has known her all his life, but she has never met this guy before. After a moment of shock, the young lady calls back.

"Oh, hi! Glad to see you could make it. C'mon its still early, we'll have some fun."

A little surprised the teacher steps back, he had thought sure the kid was only trying to make trouble. Now the young man before him shoots him a cold, devilish look and again the teacher feels threatened as the finger returns to guide itself up his back. Cold as ice this time. Josie leads the mysterious stranger to a side corridor.

"I appreciate you helping me out, though I would have gotten in either way. Anyway, my name is Seth."

"Oh yeah, it was no problem. I'm Josie Lastings, so Seth do you have a last name to go along with your first?" Josie seems to talk in a flirt like manner, a part of her feels attracted to this guy. Of course it could just be that normal teenage syndrome where every guy she meets is her dream. Oh well, we all grow out of that state don't we?

Seth looks deep into the girl's eyes and says, "Wake!" What kind of name is Seth Wake the girl thinks to herself?

"Again I thank you," Wake states as he turns to walk away. Josie feels somewhat offended, after all he would not even be in the dance if not for her.

"Hey, where are you going, do you really have someone you are meeting? I mean are you blind or what?"

Seth stops for a moment then turns back to her, "No one here is worthy of my company, unless of course they have what it is I am looking for. Then again, how would I know which one of you are the one?"

Josie can not believe what she is hearing, no one worthy, give me a break. Now her memory serves up the situation that had occurred only moments ago, somehow this guy knew her name.

"You called me Josie, how do you know who I am if we have never met before."

Seth grins a little then gives his explanation. "You do great art Ms. Lastings, I recognize you from one of the pieces you did for the Art Achievers Award."

His answer does not really seem too possible, but the young lady buys it anyhow.

"And one other thing, Seth starts, I can see very well, you are a beautiful woman. I just don't have any use for you as of now." His words are cold and insulting, though he still speaks with that same calm softness. Then he eyes her up and down. Josie stands there a little confused. Wake gestures with his tongue in such a manner it shocks her. And from that point, the guy walks off into the gym.

Josie returns to the refreshment area to rejoin Lisa and Tommy and let them know how rude this Seth Wake had been.

Inside the gymnasium, Andrea Salem (Mark Salem's daughter) sways to the sound of the music. Seth Wake stares at her from a short distance, almost in a stone like manner, not moving or blinking. She catches him eying her and begins to show off a little. Liking what he sees, Seth walks over to introduce himself.

"Your a good dancer, perhaps I could join you," he requests.

"Hmm, sounds good to me stranger, the name is Andrea , so tell me who is it I will be dancing with?" Andrea states this, curiosity running wild as she looks at the new face in front of her.

"Seth Wake, now lets dance, you could show me a move or two," Wake replies. The couple begins to move as the next song comes on and the dance rages on.

Not too far away from Andrea, Larry Stant, Kevin Spencer and Kevin Riley continue joking around. Then in the distance the three spot Tommy Critton and Lisa Mays beginning to dance. Larry Stant gets one of his great ideas and moves in on the happy couple. Josie Lastings talks with a couple guys over in the dining area paying no attention to her friends. Barry and Kevin follow close as Larry walks up to his former girlfriend.

"So may I have this dance Lisa, I mean you don't really want to continue dancing with this guy," states Larry smartly. Tommy begins to boil inside, he is sick and tired of these guys sticking their ugly ass noses in his business.

"Listen Larry, she doesn't want to dance with you, and she doesn't want to talk to you, you got that!" Tommy talks with a lot of aggression, Larry can sense it too, and likes it.

Barry Spencer once again has to put his in, "Chill out babes, we just hanging at the dance. Larry only wants to have a little fun, you know?" Stant shakes his head in agreement, Kevin Riley stays back a little ways expecting something to break out. Tommy glares at the three troublemakers then grabs Lisa's hand and leads her away. Larry, Kevin and Barry all laugh, they are pleased with what they have accomplished. Seth Wake and Andrea Salem walk passed the group, Wake stops and looks their way. Larry and the other two stop laughing and stare back. A cold chill, same as the one that reached the teachers back, now hit the three High School students.

"The strong always seem to prey on the weak, especially when the numbers are in their favor," Seth says coldly. Now he gives them a wicked grin and walks out with Andrea at his side. The two pass Tommy and Lisa on the front steps as they are leaving. Lisa glares at Wake as he walks by and then turns back to her man. They hug one another, as Seth and Andrea disappear from sight, only two chaperone's standing by the front door remain outside with the love birds.

Inside, Josie realizes she has been abandoned. It does not bother her too much though, her and James Smilot were hitting things off quite well. The two knew each other through her brother Michael who was friends with Timothy Smilot, James' older brother. Timmy and Mike had always been friends, not like best friends or anything. More like someone you would take fishing with you just so you could say you caught more fish. Over the years though, it's getting better all the time. The two friends worked together now and seemed to have a blast. Sometimes a little too much kidding around kept the guys form their work, but it was indeed fun. As James and Josie dance on, a slow song flows out of the speakers all around. James takes Josie's hand and leads her to a vacant part of the dance floor. After a brief pause, he pulls her close and the new couple begins to move to the sound of the music.

Seth and Andrea walk down the front steps then proceed to the side of the building. The black Chevrolet Blazer remains parked between two pickup trucks whose license plates go right along with the country theme in the city. Upon them read 'CWBOYUP' and 'CTRYGRL. Seth removes his keys from his pockets and walks Andrea to the passenger side of the vehicle. She hops in once the door is open and Wake returns to the driver side of the vehicle. The truck lets out a rumble as it starts up and exhaust shoots out the dual tale pipes. Seth shifts the truck into reverse and backs out. Andrea, without asking, reaches for the radio and fixes it to her favorite station. The Blazer pulls onto the main road, Wake punches it and the vehicle leaves about eight feet of tire tracks on the pavement. Andrea laughs and rubs her newfound friends arm. Wake exits the main road as soon as possible, disappearing into the winding side roads of Trench city.

"I love off- roading, what a great idea. I mean we will never get stuck in this thing." Andrea is not sure if that is really the idea or not but it does not really matter, she is having a ball. Seth smiles and continues on, straight up ahead appears a dirt road. The Blazer turns right into the muddy dirt filled path before them. Andrea laughs as the truck bounces left and right through the mud and the muck. A large hill takes the vehicle up for some ways, a drop occurs afterward but there is no way of telling at the time. Unless, that is, you knew the road already. Seth pushes onward. The truck comes off the top of the hill and becomes slightly air born landing in a great hole at the bottom of the hill. The four-wheel drive is now buried to its wheel wells. It keeps getting it at first then does nothing but spin. Wake shifts to reverse only to find more of the same. With out any other choice, Seth switches to four-wheel drive. Now the truck moves forward again almost making it out. The weight shifts and the truck slides in the mud, it sinks dangerously low on the passenger side and the Blazer stops moving. Andrea holds her breath, its pitch black out here in the woods and they are stuck?

No, Seth would get them out she thought. The young man shifts to reverse again then back to drive. The truck seems to be going nowhere. Wake presses down a little farther on the gas though not as much as he probably should have. Andrea tries not to let the smirk on her face be too obvious, after all she does not want her friend to think she knows what is really happening.

Seemingly disgusted, he throws the vehicle into park and kills the motor. Andrea plays along. "Are we really stuck?" Though she knows the answer she would receive, and maybe she wants the answer as much as he does. Seth is a great looking guy, so what if he isn't that great at the old running out of gas trick.

"Yeah, the ol girl is actually letting me down. Man, I cant believe how quiet and dark it is out here. If you like I will keep the headlights on along with the interior. Maybe someone will see us and come help."

"O.K., that sounds great, and I guess we will just wait here in the truck huh?" Andrea squeezed Seth's hand and he brings it to his lips. Next the two move a little closer together, neither really sure of what to do next.

From out of the darkness comes a loud crunching sound. It seems to be just outside the vehicle. Andrea's heart could have stopped. Wake doesn't seem scared at all though. He puts his finger up as if to say, wait a second. Then he begins to open the truck door. Whatever it is outside the vehicle, he would simply scare away and that would be that. He grunts a bit as he hoists himself down from the truck, which if it were any other vehicle would really be stuck. Andrea hears his footsteps go to the rear of the vehicle, then they stop and he lets out a small yell. Everything goes silent. Scared to death now, Andrea Salem quickly grabs the driver side door and pulls it shut. A growl comes from the midst of the night. The girl curls up in her seat and barely holds in a squeal. In seconds the beast leaps from the ground to the hood of the truck. It's bloody fangs show in the moonlight as it lets out another growl. The noise that they had thought as nothing earlier now turned out to be a huge gray wolf. Andrea screams in horror as the beast howls into the night. Another wolf smashes into the passenger side door followed by yet a third that screeches its nails down the back window. Tears rolled down the young ladies face as the gray wolfs head smashes through the windshield, Andrea passes out from pure fright!

Chapter 7

A FEW MILES AWAY, MICHAEL Lastings grows closer to his house as he has recently finished up his grocery shopping. He rubs the sleep from his eyes then drops his speed about ten miles an hour. He takes a glance in the rear view mirror, flashing lights appear behind him. First Michael thinks it to be a cop, one of those who has had a bad night and wants someone else to share it. But it is an ambulance, not a cop. Quickly he lowers his speed once again and pulls to the side of the road. The ambulance shoots by him causing Michael's vehicle to waver a slight bit. Now the boy pulls back on the road and takes chase. Curiosity killed the cat, maybe, but this cat only wants the satisfaction of knowing what is happening. Catching up to the emergency vehicle is a little bit of a task, Lastings enjoys the challenge. They come to the city limits and keep on getting it. As the flashing lights pass Caroline's restaurant it takes a right and continues on for a couple more blocks. It turns onto a street by the name of Castleplain Dr. then joins three police cars and a fire truck three houses down. For a moment Michael had become weary as the ambulance had turned as if to go into his sisters place of employment, it passed quickly. Now an uneasy feeling sweeps over him, and he feels the cold fingers crawling up his back. He parks a couple houses down, pushes the vehicle into park, and then watches on. Two cops stand on the porch talking to a familiar face, Michael does not know from where quite yet. The lady looks to be hysterical, the cops can barely make out the words as she explains how she had found her fallen lover. Michael's jaw falls as the person comes to him, Susan Falls, Susan Falls that works with Josie at Caroline's. The boy does not know what to expect, what could have happened? His answer comes sooner than later, two EMT's come out of the small one story house carrying a body bag. Lastings can not believe his eyes, he feels so sorry for Susan. Unfortunately he does not dare add to the scene. It must have been some horrible accident, or maybe something worse. Michael has seen enough, he takes the needle down to drive and pulls away, intending to be home as quick as possible. The Mustang speeds on, heading for Lastings house no more than a mile away. Hundreds of thoughts run through Michael's head, could Susan Falls' husband have been killed, is that why the police were there? No, they would have shown up either way, standard procedure and all. Then that face appears in his mind, not because he wants it to, it has been placed here. Those fangs, those eyes, and what about the crazy words he had spoke? This same guy has killed Susan's husband, now it seems definite. The words ring out again, only Michael can not remember them, somehow they just come to him.

"You may see them by night, when the moon beams full over the valley, which shall smell of death."

As the words boom inside his head, a cold sweat runs down his face. Yes, he had killed him, Michael knew it. Did it not all add up, or does accusing a man of murder for a few mysterious words and fangs for teeth go a little too far? Michael can not be sure what to think at this point. One thing can be sure though, he would be keeping these thoughts to himself.

Back at the high school, the Autumn Dance will soon be coming to an end. Josie Lastings, James Smilot, Lisa Mays and Tommy

Critton prepare to exit the building. First they stop by the pay phones to give their parents a call and fill them in on what plans are.

"I had a lot of fun James, see you Monday O.K.. Oh, and thanks for a great dance", Josie speaks with a very sincere tone. She truly had enjoyed herself. In the back of her mind though she wishes it had been Craig she had been dancing with.

James answers quickly, "No problem, but hey, why don't you let me take you home? I mean if that is all right with Tommy and Lisa. They could always ride home with her parents, or maybe if Tommy drove himself..."

"Great", Josie exclaimed interrupting her date for the night. He smiled then both said good-bye and left Lisa and Tommy to themselves.

"I know your parents were real exited about bringing you to the dance, and well, I did not mind meeting you here, but can I take you out for a little while? And then maybe a little later take you home, you know, the way we did last year?" Tommy looked to almost be begging, Lisa knew better though, he was not the type.

"Well, I suppose you could have the pleasure of taking me out, and then home later, much later that is!"

Tommy laughs pulling his girl against him and kissing her on the forehead. "All right then, let's go call your parents and get going huh?"

Lisa Mays shakes her head yes, then both move into the front hall. Larry Stant makes a point to glare at the two as they walk by, they ignore him and continue outside not realizing Stant and his goons follow close behind. Larry has other things in mind than the two having a good time the rest of the night. He has remained constantly jealous since the breakup. Of course he tells his friends he does not care either way, he just likes to mess with Tommy.

Outside, the temperature has dropped considerably. The wind blows fiercely against the faces of Tommy and Lisa. Lisa shivers as the cool night air shoots up against her. She makes the phone call to her parents as quick as possible. They have no problem with her going out and spending most the rest of the night with Tommy, after all, at least they don't have to put up with Larry Stant. Everyone agrees for young Lisa to be in by two am., so Tommy walks her to the car. Larry Stant's voice yells out from behind them.

"Yo Tommy, the dance aint over yet, where are you two love birds going?" Behind him stands Barry Spencer and Kevin Riley. These guys are like a pack, very seldom did you catch one alone. The three guys now join Tommy at his vehicle. Tommy feels its time to make a stand, if not these three would never leave him alone.

"Listen, I am getting real tired of you three following me around. Now just get the hell out of here. This is our time and it is none of your business what we do now, or even a week from now." Tommy's voice is sharp and stern.

"No need to get yourself all worked up boy, we's just funning with you, right Larry," Kevin says smartly.

"Ha, I just wanted to wish you fun tonight. I am sure you and your bitch are gonna make each other squeal!" Larry's words sting Tommy, he can't stand the sound of his voice.

"We're leaving Larry, Tommy fires back. Now, get out of here, you are not welcome around Lisa!" Tommy slowly but surely loses his patience more and more by the second. Lisa looks on worriedly, shivering in the hard wind.

"Just make sure she gives you some head Tommy, trust me, I know first hand, she can give some good head," Larry teases, his two goons behind him laugh! Lisa shrinks back trying to hide her face. She hates him, how could he say something like that?"

Tommy's blood boils, that was it, the breaking point. Critton clenches his fists in a silent rage. The three guys in front of him laugh on, not for long though. Without another word, the angry young man tears into Larry Stant. This was it, he couldn't take it anymore, and it was time for this son of a bitch to get what's coming to him. A strong left hook to the jaw drops the bully like a bad habit. It happens so quick that his two friends hesitate before reacting. Kevin Riley moves in, Tommy turns to him and brings his leg up. Riley doubles over, the shot hit him right where it counts, and a moment later he joins Larry on the ground. Barry Spencer has time to prepare, he wraps his hand in the chain that leads from his wallet to his pants. As Tommy changes direction to face his third on comer, Barry plasters him with his right fist. Poor Tommy never sees it coming. A sickening thud rings out as the wrapped fist connects with Tommy's face. Lisa screams and runs to her man's side. Spencer pushes her aside and proceeds to kick the young man while he is down. Finally Larry and Kevin get back to their feet and the three run off. Tommy Critton lies on the cold asphalt, a bloody mess. His entire body feels numb. The pain seems almost unbearable, Tommy can feel the warm blood run down his face. His nose and mouth have been busted wide open. Strangely enough, the warm blood almost feels good running down the fallen Tommy's face. It seems to be the only warm part of his body. Lisa Mays sits with him, crying hysterically, hoping that help will soon arrive. A couple teachers run over a few minutes later, they send another student in to contact the medical squad. Barry Spencer would be in allot of trouble once the cops catch up to him. As for the others, you know what they say, what goes around comes around.

Chapter 8

THE BIRDS BEGIN TO sing as the sun stretches out, sending rays of light upon the earth. Derek Lastings lies still asleep on the couch. After forty-five minutes of trying to get him up, Jennifer had left him for the night. A loud thud form the arriving Sunday paper wakes him with a start. After shaking the cobwebs and realizing what the noise was, Derek decides to go ahead and get up. Thoughts of the night before come to mind, had his daughter even come home, or could she still be out gallivanting. A little wearily Mr. Lastings makes his way to the bottom of the stairs and begins to climb them. After a quick peep in on his daughter and a sigh of relief, the man returns to the first floor. The clock on the wall reads seven a.m., he begins to wonder why he decided to get up after all. Discreetly as possible Lastings sneaks out on the porch to grab the morning paper, all the while doing his best not to wake anyone in the process. He closes the door behind him then takes his seat back on the couch. With the flip of a switch the small lamp on the in table beams on. Derek Lastings has to look twice at the print on the front page.

Unknown killer remains at large after leaving one dead, just beyond Trench city limits!

With eyes now wide-open and mixed emotion plaguing his mind, Derek looks to the rest of the article.

Robert Falls was found dead yesterday in his own home after an apparent intruder took his life with one cut to the throat, this undoubtedly the man's demise.

The more Derek reads, the less he can believe it. Something like this had not happened within ten miles of Trench in over fifteen years. That had been a time when some poor ladies lover went crazy and killed her and then turned the gun on himself. Lastings looks on.

On a more eerie note, a single drinking glass found on the kitchen counter had been stained with blood.

This just keeps getting crazier, Derek thinks to himself, curiosity burns as he read more.

When asked about such an unusual event, the police gave no comment. Now more than ever you have to wonder, did the vampires really die out hundreds of years ago?

Derek stops reading here, what in the hell did that mean? Of course the vampires were extinct. There had been no attacks since the early seventeen hundreds and in the eighteenth century, all had believed to have captured the worlds last remaining vamp! A headache begins to tear at Lastings brain. Movement out of the corner of his eye causes him to jump until it turns out to be his wife. She stands there in the door way obviously half asleep.

"Reading the paper already Derek, c'mon, Sunday is one of your days to sleep in."

Derek says nothing at first, only continues to stare at the front page, *vampires.* No way!

"A man has been murdered, only a few blocks away from Caroline's restaurant." His words come out monotone, no feeling at all, apparently this has come as quite a shock. Although, the situation at hand would rock any small city like that of Trench!

"What? That's where Josie works, oh my God!" Thoughts of her little girl being the one it had happened to did not take long to enter her imagination. She walks over to her husband attempting to grab the paper. Derek grips it tightly but does turn it slightly so his wife can read the fine print. Surprise crawls onto her face, slowly though, like one of those water bulbs with the snow inside that falls when you turn it upside down to right side up. They stare at each other in a silent horror. A knock on the door breaks the silence. Derek gets up to answer it as his wife runs into the bedroom to cover herself better. She had only been wearing a skimpy pink nightgown, one that revealed her chest quite well. Had the man she loves not been shaking by the paper it could have led to a bit of early morning lust. Fortunately that is not what happened. The door opens to reveal a police officer waiting on the other side. He lets the man in and asks what he can do for him.

"I am looking for, a Josie Lastings. It seems a young lady from her school has disappeared and it is possible Josie can help us out a little." The officer stands quite tall and has a very husky figure. Derek figures the guy could most likely bench press a small two-passenger car. The name on the badge reads Foyle.

"I'm not quite sure what is going on here, but I assure you my daughter will do anything she can to help. She is asleep right now, I will just be a minute to wake her"

"I would appreciate it Mr. Lastings, you see, your daughter seems to know the boy that was last seen with our missing person." Foyle wanted to explain himself, and wanted to be discreet at the same time. The steps slightly creak on the way up as Derek went off to wake Josie. A knock on the door causes her to stir a bit, then a second gets an answer.

"Just, just a minute, "Josie stutters. her father waits tentatively outside the door. She slips on a robe and opens up.

"There is an officer downstairs, he says you might be able to help because you were one of the last to see a student that has come up missing." Derek talks with a lot of weariness in his voice, still not quite sure of what is going on. Josie rolls her eyes and shuts the door, she would get dressed and come down in a few minutes. Her dad knew the girl would be right out, so her turns away, back downstairs to the officer.

"She will be down in a moment, just has to slip some clothes on." The policeman shakes his head and continues waiting, very patiently at that. Five to ten minutes went by, the sound of a door opening can be heard from upstairs. Josie Lastings then appears at the doorstep, she pauses a moment then continues on.

"Josie hi, I am Officer Foyle. Last night you helped a young man get into the dance by saying he was with you, I hope you could give me his name. He, nor our lost student has been seen since yesterday evening." The way Foyle talked, Josie felt like she could be a criminal or something.

"Well, Josie said, his name was very strange to me. Not one you would here everyday. And I only helped him get into the dance cause I thought her was cute, he turned out to be a jerk. Oh, do not forget pervert, the guy made tongue gestures at me, what nerve!"

"Yes ma'am, but did you get his name, can you remember it." He seemed irritated, the patience from earlier slowly left him.

Josie tensed up, "Yes, it is Seth, Seth Wake."

"Seth Wake huh, well is there anything else you can tell me, we have two missing person's here, whatever you know could help"

Josie answers, "No, I'm sorry. Nothing else to tell. I helped the guy into the dance, and he acts like I do not even exist. So then he licks his lips to me like I am some sort of treat. Some gratitude if you ask me. Anyway, then he got all wrapped up with Andrea, that is all I know."

"So you did see him with Andrea Salem, that is good to know. And you have nothing else? O.K., then I will be on my way."

Derek Lastings speaks up, "Officer Foyle, you said the girls parents reported her missing, what of the boy?"

"Strangely enough no one has called about him, which technically means he is not a missing person, he could very well be a suspect. But, we talked to the teachers who attended the dance, that's where we got our information. The man I spoke with informed us that the girl, Andrea, was last seen with this Seth guy. Whom Josie Lastings let in the door saying he was with her. From that point we had no choice cept to come here and see what your daughter knew."

"All right well thank you for your time officer, maybe you could give us a ring when the girl turns up."

"Yes, of course," Foyle answers, then turns to leave. Josie goes back to her room to get a little more rest before its time for work. Derek and Jennifer put on some coffee to hopefully wake themselves up. Soon thereafter, Brad Lastings comes stumbling in from the bedroom. The kid woke up a little early this morning, Jennifer gives him a morning kiss then sits him down for a bowl of cereal. Bradford waits impatiently for his breakfast, then pulls out a half melted bag of M&M's from his pocket.

When Derek returns from the kitchen with a cup of Joe, the boy begins throwing the candy in his father's direction laughing hysterically the whole time.

While Derek Lastings fights to keep his youngest son from making a mess of the house, Michael lies still in bed. The twenty one year old has his eyes wide open staring blankly at the ceiling. What he had seen the night before stuck in his head, the body bag coming out of the house, Susan standing on the porch hysterical. A bird flutters by the window and Michael receives a slight scare. He decides it is time for a bite to eat, the young man jumps out of bed and walks to the kitchen. Upon finding a box of Cream of Wheat, he begins to mix it up. In less than a minute, he thinks to himself letting out a chuckle. The house stands very quiet, only the sound of his Nascar clock ticking with the seconds can be heard. Michael likes it this way, it gives him a feeling of peace. A visitor seems to cut him short of finishing the bowl of creamy wheat. As the door is unlatched and the dead bolt slid over, he opens the door. To Lastings horror, the man on the other side is the exact one him and his friends had seen at the basketball court. Michael freezes, stunned to see this eerie being on his own front door step. The man we have now come to know as Ambrose grins and prepares to enter the house. Young Lastings legs begin to feel like rubber , almost as if they will collapse beneath him. He walks backwards away from the man before him. Suddenly Ambrose hisses, revealing his razor sharp fangs. Michael Lastings falls to the floor, almost as if a giant wind has swept him from his feet and left him to lie on his back. Ambrose begins to move in, Michael gets to his feet and runs for his bedroom. He can almost feel cold breath on the back of his neck as his assailant follows. He runs into the room quickly slamming and locking the door. A bow and arrow sit in the closet, Michael thinks twice about it before removing it. It is not exactly hunting season now, though just the same he has an animal to kill. A loud crash from the outside of the door removes it half off its hinges. Then a second kick from Ambrose causes the door to splinter from the wall and fall to the floor. Michael pulls back and lets an arrow soar, it digs deep into Ambrose's gut, sending him flailing to the floor. It is not over though, breath still flows strongly in and out of the man's body. Michael sets another arrow to fly and waits for his opponent to return to his feet. Ambrose seems to fly back to a standing position, the arrow shoots. This time it never finds its mark as the unholy being catches it and turns it on Michael. The point cuts into the young mans chest as it is shoved forward. He falls to his knees now at the mercy of Ambrose. Michael's eyes seem to glaze over as the man before him opens his mouth revealing once again the fangs with in. As the pointed teeth dig into Michael Lastings neck, everything goes black.

"Aagh!" Michael screams as he shot awake from his horrible dream. Sweat spews from his brow and each breath comes short and fast. He looks all around the room frantically looking for the evil man that had appeared in his dreams. A little relief can be found here since there is no one!

Chapter 9

ELSEWHERE, EUGENE BROWDER SITS scaling fish he had caught almost a week before. The man lives alone, his wife and kids were killed over ten years ago in a fatal car accident. All the man has now is his fishing, and his mechanical work. Browder finishes up on the last striper then tosses it over with the rest of the pile. Upon washing his hands, Eugene picks up the bucket full of fish and moves it in to the bathtub. As for the heads and skins of the fish, he would dispose of them later. The bathtub slowly fills itself with hot water, now the bucket of scaled fish becomes dumped into the steamy water below. Soon the fish would be ready to cook. Eugene stands up to go for another container stored in his back room off of the kitchen. As he turns a corner, his own fish scaler becomes lodged in his chest. Immense pain flows through his whole body, Browder drops to his knees. Ash looks down on him, his eyes burn with evil. Then the vampire pulls Eugene back to his feet staring him right in the eyes. The pain continues to be too much, Browder can do nothing. His thoughts run wild, this is the end, and this is what death feels like.

The man could feels the life seeping out of his body. Ash ends it, burying his teeth into the neck of his fallen prey. Blood is sucked into the mouth of a seemingly inhuman Ash! Eugene is dropped lifelessly to the rug-covered floor below.

Right next door, Steven Mass, one of Michael's good friends has called the police. He had watched Ash enter his neighbor's house uninvited. Steven looks on from his front window as the prowler steps outside and pulls the door closed behind him. It would still be a few minutes before the cops arrived, Mass feels obligated to take matters into his own hands. His father always kept a loaded gun locked in the cabinet. Steven never did understand why, you don't need a loaded gun in a town like Trench. Now though, he was thankful. After retrieving the key from the wall hook, the want to be hero nervously removes a rifle from the gun rack. Taking a deep breath, Steve runs out of the house to try and hold off Eugene's attacker. Ash stops where he is when he hears the rifle cock behind him.

"I don't know you, but I do know you don't belong in my neighbors house. So just don't move and all will be fine. The cops are on the way, please do not make me use this." Steven warns.

Ash turns to meet the eyes of this distraction, then takes one step forward. Mass grips the weapon tightly.

"Don't, Don't move all right. Were both scared here, I realize that. B, But don't get stupid O.K.. This is a situation that does not have to escalate. Please mister, I would hate to shoot you." Steven almost pleads with the man before him. Fear could be seen all over his face. Ash on the other hand remains extremely calm.

"Steven, you're the only one scared here. You can leave any time you like. Or, you can let me taste your warm blood as it trickles down my throat." Ash says his words firmly, they dig into Steven's nerves, causing him to begin shaking. Now Ash again takes a step forward, then another, and another. Steve tightens his finger on the trigger, he does not want to shoot, but will if forced to. Ash takes to the air, almost as if he grows wings and beams towards Mass. The rifle fires, Ash crashes into the man holding the gun. Sharp, talon like finger nails dig into Steven's shoulders, then both arms go limp. Steven shoves the beast off of him then struggles to his feet. He holds the rifle still in the direction of the fallen being. Ash looks up grinning devilishly, Steven is too stunned to act as the vampire returns to his feet. Blood runs from the hip and thigh of Ash's body, it seems to be of little pain. Finally the police turn the corner up the road, Ash spins around to take notice then flees in the opposite direction of the patrol car. Two cops exit the vehicle and begin to take chase, back up also would be on its way. Sgt. Macon radios in reporting they could have Robert Falls' killer. Police from neighboring towns race quickly to join the chase. Ash heads for the trees not too far from his present area, once in the forest the cops would never be able to catch up. Only yards before reaching freedom, a car marked Trench police cuts the man off. Ash changes direction as now four cops are upon him.

"Freeze or we'll shoot, freeze or we will shoot!" calls Sgt. Macon. It would be to no avail though, the four men in blue now were forced to open fire. Ash stumbles as the bullets rip into his skin, next he falls to the hard pavement covered by that of his red cape. The officers look on at the clump of human being under the blood stained cloak. Little do they know, the thing under the cloak is hardly a normal being. Steven Mass watches on from behind, a good distance from the action. He has lowered his rifle and left the police to do their jobs. A lump catches in the boy's throat as he realizes he knows it still is not over. No movement can be seen as the cops move in, then, with in the blink of an eye,a white wolf leaps from beneath the cape. With the element of surprise very much on it's side, Ash easily escapes into the forest leaving the cops and Steven behind him, shocked!

It has just passed midday, back at Tommy Critton's house, he lay still in bed. The guy's face still aches horribly due to the events of the night before. Needless to say, him and Lisa never did finish their plans for the night. No, Tommy spent the time he should have been rolling around with his girl, in a hospital bed. Critton lives with his older sister, Tara, who currently works to fix him a good lunch. He had moved from his parent's house to get out of firing range. Having two parents who argue like cat's and dog's one minute, then screw each others brains out the next, did have its disadvantages.

Since he had moved out, the relationship between them had become stronger. Tara had contacted them to let them know about the fight, they sent best wishes, and that pretty much did it. Tommy's doctor had told him he had a slight concussion and bruised facial tissues. Then gave him two days in bed. Shoot, the young man had not made it one and already it is driving him nuts. Tommy looks over at the book that lays on his desk, Storm of the Century by Stephen King, indeed his favorite author. Even though his head seems to be killing him, he picks up the book to read, not the greatest idea in the world considering a concussion. Anyway, he picks up the book and turns to part three, The Reckoning, and begins to read. Every few moments a pain would shoot through the side of his head and face, he would bear it, then continue on. So far the book had been extremely intriguing, Tommy could not wait to see what the end would bring. Moments later, his sister Tara walks in and sets a plate at his bedside, along with a tall glass of soda. Tommy stuffs his face as he continues to read on, he takes a sip from his drink then reaches for a handful of potato chips. Tara watches on as her brother holds the chips in one hand and his book in the other.

"Since you obviously could care less that reading is the last thing you should be doing, are you not worried about getting the book all greasy? I mean, you might put it down long enough to eat." She laughs a bit.

"Good idea sis." Tommy sits the book down and grabs his plate preparing to finish his lunch. The ringing of the phone chimes from the other room. Tara quickly races off to get it.

"Hello!" she calls as she picks up the receiver. The voice on the other end asks for Tommy, it sounds to be Lisa, she thinks. Back into the other room she goes, she waits patiently as her brother slurps down more of his drink, then hands him the phone.

"Hi Lis, how is it going?"

"Better than yourself, my face is not broke into a hundred pieces. Haha. I'm just kidding dear, how are you making it? Is everything all right?"

"Well, he starts, it still hurts like hell, but I am dealing with it as best as possible. I wish I could get a hold of Barry Spencer, hurt or not I want his ass!"

Lisa giggles a little, "You don't have to worry about him, he has been charged with assault and may be spending some time in jail, he is eighteen you know? Unfortunately, the others are off scotch free. Listen, I am really sorry about all this. I mean it feels like you're laying there in bed cause of me, cause I went out with that jerk."

"Spencer could get jail time huh, well that is definitely something I like to hear. As for it being your fault, just forget about it. I am the one who started the fight so if it is anyone's fault, it is my own. What in the hell was I thinking trying to take on three guys anyway. Oh well, I did pretty well until that son of a bitch hit me with that damn chain. You know what, I should not be talking like that around you. Why don't you just come on over and we will forget about everything except each other."

"O.K., my parents will bring me, meanwhile you keep your butt in bed. You better listen to your doctor or you will have to deal with me." Lisa speaks as firmly and as menacingly as she can, barely containing her laughter.

"Yeah, yeah, I'm shaking so bad, frightened beyond belief. Now get over here. I love you!" A pain shoots through Tommy's head once again, he grimaces in agony. Lisa picks up on this and decides it time to hang up.

"See you in a few minutes, try and get a little rest until I get there." speaks Lisa convincingly. Critton says good-bye and hangs the phone up as he lays his head back to try and ease the pain. He knows Lisa, and a few minutes usually mean a few hours.

Derek Lastings looks at his watch, it reads quarter till one o'clock. Currently he is putting together a tool shed. It becomes more of a task every passing moment. Then again whenever his son Bradford is around, that's how things turn out. The kid continues to run off with his tools. The little kid brings back a hammer, only to grab a screwdriver and run off again. Inside, Jennifer has now finished telling Josie about Robert Falls. The girl did not know him personally, but her and Susan talked allot. A blank look rests on

Josie's pretty face, she does not know what to say. Andrea had come up missing with this Seth guy, and now Susan's husband had been killed. Jennifer comforts her daughter, not really wanting her to work her shift that night any more. The back door shuts as Derek brings young Brad in kicking and screaming. Next he sets the boy in a chair and turns to his wife. "Please keep him in here, I can't get any work done this way." explains Derek.

Jennifer rolls her eyes but agrees to his wishes. She grabs Brad as he begins to follow his father back outside.

Josie goes upstairs to try and analyze the situation. She feels a little scared to go into work, though at the same rate feels obligated to since Susan would obviously be in no shape to work for quite some time. Someone had to help out. The girl stares as a bug crawls up the wall, pretending she did not see it. A second later she jumps up and turns the radio on attempting to forget about it all.

While the Lastings deal with there own problems, Mark and Patricia Salem sit waiting, wondering if they would ever see precious Andrea again. They have no idea who Seth Wake is, or if he could be the reason she came up missing. Mark does his best to console his wife as she sobs lightly. He had become as worried as she at this point, only he did his best not to let it show too much. The sound of a doorbell comes and the Salem's look at one another. Mark gets up to answer the door. This would be the third time the cops had shown up after Andrea had been reported missing. The officer is invited in and he begins to explain what has been found.

"Mr. and Mrs. Salem, I wish I could tell you the condition of your daughter at this point, only we do not know as of yet. On the other hand, Seth Wake's truck has been found off in the woods. Apparently the two got stuck in the mud. From there, we have no idea. Now, please don't jump to conclusions, but the truck had been slightly torn up. The windshield has been busted and spots of blood found on the passenger side seat. And as far as the where abouts of Andrea and Seth Wake now, again, we don't know, I'm sorry."

Patricia now cries hysterically, nothing Mark can do will help. Her baby is missing, possibly the young girl has been kidnapped. The cop does not know what else to say, that is all they have right now. Mr. Salem thanks him for his time, and the officer leaves seconds later.

Meanwhile, the Salem's poor daughter lay face down on a leaf covered forest floor. Blood runs from her many wounds, the wolves had left her in pretty bad shape. Now she wakes about three and a half miles from where the truck sat. The girl is still alive, barely conscious though. Andrea wants to get off the ground, she tries bravely and finds she does not have the strength to do so. Next, sunshine of hope comes to her, the sound of footsteps can be heard only yards away. That had to be footsteps, or maybe, maybe it is the wolves coming back to finish her. Yes, this is it. They would tear away at her flesh, and chew on her rotten carcass for weeks to come. Wait, a person came to sight, she slowly lifts her head to look up. She finds a familiar sight. Seth Wake kneels down beside her, not a scratch can be seen on him. Andrea does not notice. She feels safe now, yes, safe.

"Glad to find you finally awake Andrea, I thought you were done for. Thankfully you are all right, well, almost." Seth says with some roughness in his voice. He puts his arm around Andrea and lifts the girl to her feet. She cannot stand alone, so she holds onto Seth with all that's in her. Wake takes his pointer and middle finger and wipes a bit of blood from Salem's arm, touching it to his tongue.

"Sweet inside and out, as I thought. It's not right though, no you are not the one." These words sound Greek to the wounded girl, she thinks nothing of it and the two continue on. It takes some time with Andrea injured, but eventually they make it to a main road. Seth lays his girl down to flag a passing vehicle, she needs to get to a hospital. Larry Bora, who we met earlier, helps get Andrea into the back seat of the car. Her eyes swell up with tears, the pain is too great to handle. She moans as the car pulls off the side of the road. Trench does not have it's own hospital, so they have to go to Spontania, a neighboring city. Seth explains everything to Larry Bora on the way to the hospital. The sun glares in Bora's eyes as it sets on the horizon. The man removes his prescription sunglasses from the case and puts them on. The Chrysler engine roars as it reaches the speed of sixty-five. Larry holds it here, soon Andrea would be in good hands. As for Mr. and Mrs. Salem, they would know they're daughter is safe.

Elsewhere, Ash and Ambrose meet in a bearing valley. The wounds that Ash has received are all but gone amazingly. Ambrose tends to the remaining shots, then he stops. Both men look to the sky, the view of cave walls cloud they're vision. Then a swarm of bats exiting a dark crevice come into sight.

"Father calls to us Ash." Ambrose informs. Ash nods his head. Both men turn ruggedly pail, hair begins to extrude from all parts of the body, soon a white and gray wolf replace the two human forms. The wolves trot away in the direction of the water. Here they would turn into bats. Then both would ride the winds to the island where Abraham awaits them.

Chapter 10

THE WATER HAS SETTLED around the island, only small waves crash against the shore. A gentle breeze rolls over the jagged rocks that surround the body of land. Ash and his brother Ambrose stand at the highest peak of the rock formation atop the island. They peer out over the water before them. It is crystal clear, and you can see as far down as your eyes will take you. The sun has begun its timely downward descent as the day draws to an end. Not wanting to keep Abraham waiting, the two men climb down from the peak and disappear into the shadowy caves. The scene is as before, a lamp on a single rock, and thousands of cobwebs. The old gray haired man that is Abraham appears from out of the blackness.

"Three hundred years have passed since the death of my wife. The woman died trying to receive the exact item in which you search for, the rare blood type. As I turned the year of eighty-two, my father told me of a way to be young again. Though it had been too late for him, I could still take it for myself. Instead, I went on without it, feeling my age was still young for our kind. My actions were foolish, for something of such power comes only every three hundred years.

At three centuries plus eighty-two years, the time came again. Now at a great mature age, I set out to take what was mine. It was not to be though, a fatal wound almost ended my life and ruined all chances of once again capturing the blood. So we come to the incredible age of six hundred and eighty two. All I accomplish this time is the marrying of my wife Alise. Twenty years after, she sets out see if there is still a chance, for she knows my age will be much next time around. It is very unfortunate, she is killed on trying to do so. And now, in my final years, I have this absolute last chance. As you know my age is well over that of nine centuries, I am weak and near powerless if I leave this place. Now here on the other hand, I am still most powerful, but my days are numbered. All is not lost though, for one hundred and seventy years ago, you two were brought to me by that of a boat wreck. With my powers at their greatest here inside these walls, I turned you to my own kind. You must venture forth and take what is ours from whomever or whatever has it, my time is limited." Abraham bows his head, the old age plagues his body.

"Yes father, we will capture it for you father. And With the help of Seth there is no stopping the three of us. And when we find the blood type, we will all be young again and have a great feast." Ash says.

Abraham looks at Ambrose. "You must stay close to Ash and the two of you will be strong together. Do not leave him again as you did today."

Upon finishing his sentence, Abraham turns and starts his lazy climb back to the cave ceiling above. Ash and Ambrose exit, then from the shadows two black bats circle the island, then disappear into what is now a night sky. Clouds make it even darker than usual, the moon cannot be seen. The city of Trench has become quiet and seemingly empty. Most of the city goers have turned in for the night, for the hardest day of the week would soon be upon them.

It is now the dead of night, Michael Lastings clock reads twenty after three. While all the other residents sleep soundly, poor Mike stares empty eyed, though not in any one direction. The nightmare that he had endured the morning before plays over and over in his mind. Soon he decides sleep is all but hopeless. Michael decides a midnight snack would be great, or even an after midnight snack would do. So he slowly crawls his way out of bed, almost stumping his toe on the dresser, and proceeds in for a treat. Tucked into the cupboard lays a box of chocolate twins snack cakes, he shuffles a couple from the box then pours a glass of milk. Nightmares never bothered Michael Lastings this bad before, normally he could forget all about it. Only one other time had he been up like this because of a dream. This had been years ago when he and some friends witnessed a fatal car wreck. The girl in the passenger seat of one car sprang from the windshield and landed with a splat, rolling round and round, then came to a dead stop. After that, for a whole week, Lastings dreamed this poor girl had been his sister, and he watched her as her poor mangled body slowly came to a rolling stop. Blood splattered everywhere she had touched along the way. It finally went away though, what a relief that was. This nightmare now had been just the same, too real, and just like it had really happened. Michael takes another bite of his early morning goody, then begins to stare at a plaque on his wall. He had won this years ago while still attending school, this is how it reads.

> *This award is presented to Michael S. Lastings for excellent achievement in all classes, keep up the good work.*

Below these words you can see a book and ruler etched in gold. Those were the days he thought, when the mind was all that counted. Michael had always been a quick learner, now he felt as if it were all for nothing.

Right outside the house came the sound of a twig snapping and leaves rustling. Lastings train of thought quickly jumped back to reality, his eyes found the phone on the wall. Would it be absurd to call his parents, or better, the police? Michael stands up and draws open the curtains, his heart pounding. Only darkness flows in through the window. Paranoia runs over the young adult, he just knows its the man from his nightmare, from the basketball court. Something had to be done, Michael did his best to clear his head of all negative thoughts. Then he took a flash light from his own personal junk drawer, come on, everybody has one, and flips it on. The beam of light hits against the houses front door. All locks remain in place, until Michael slowly unlatches them, pulling the door open. No one or thing can be seen yet, Lastings exits the house and begins to the back of his house. He can feel eyes upon him, he can feel someone watching him. A shadow catches his eye, just beyond the rear corner of the house. Putting fear behind him, Michael takes chase, casting the light immediately in that direction. Something had been there, the young man runs after it. As he turns the corner of his house, he runs slam into his propane tank, he screams and jumps back. He breathes heavily, and his heart throbs as if to come right out of his chest. Moments later, after gathering himself, he realizes it had been nothing and returns inside. He locks the door behind him . The night continues on, eventually Michael passes out on the couch, similar to his father earlier. Soon day is again upon us, and all too soon for Derek Lastings son.

The beginning of the week once again rages its ugly head. Derek groans as his alarm sounds, he hits snooze then lies back down again. A few more minutes, he thinks, it can't be Monday morning already. Ten more minutes go by and the alarm sounds again, this time Derek turns it plain off. A few more minutes come and go, Jennifer Lastings sits up in bed.

"Your not going back to sleep are you honey?" his wife exclaims startling him slightly.

"No I'm up." Derek grunts pulling himself out of bed. He now has thirty minutes to get to work, if he skips breakfast, he might just make it. As the man readies himself to leave, the sound of voices, or maybe the sound of one voice whispering can be heard. Walking into the living room, Derek finds his daughter Josie talking on the phone. He shakes his head and clears his voice. The girl looks up like a deer caught in headlights.

"It is six thirty Josie, who are you talking to? No, never mind, just get off the phone." Anger can be heard in the man's voice.

"Dad, I am talking to James, can't I stay on a little longer?" Josie pleads.

"No, no, no, I don't even know how long you have been talking already. This is ridiculous, did you even go to bed last night?"

Josie shakes her head yes, and begins to get off the phone. Her dad turns on the news as he finishes preparing for work.

"Two deaths in two days. That's the top story in Trench this morning. The bodies of Robert Falls and Eugene Browder were both found just moments after their deaths." announces the newsman of television. Derek has the volume on low, but these words seem to boom in his ears. The reporter continues.

"Police seem to think both were killed by the same man. We also have reports of very mysterious findings at both crime scenes. A glass stained with blood has been recovered from the counter of Falls' home. And with Browder something much more disturbing. A single vicious bite to the man's throat has to strike fear into us all. But there is more, a fish scaler had been shoved into the man's chest only moments before."

People of Trench, I dare say it has been hundreds of years since we seen the last of the night crawlers and walkers. Could it be one still remains after all these years? Well, witnesses say yes. One man reports to have watched the police chase our killer, saying the man transformed in to a wolf and disappeared into the forest."

The more Lastings hears, the closer he listens. Josie sits only feet away almost quivering in fright, though Derek's attention is shown elsewhere.

"When asked about these reports, police gave no comment. Now I will agree with you viewers, that's the craziest thing I have ever heard. But again, believe the witness about the wolf or not, a killer is still on the loose. We will have more on this matter later, now we have to go to a short break. We will return with your morning forecast."

Derek and Josie Lastings seem hypnotized by the television. Though a commercial ad now shows on the picture tube, it is the news reporter they both still hear and see. It takes some time, then Mr. Lastings finally snaps out of it and hits the power button on the control. He looks at his daughter, she no longer holds the phone in her hand. Now the girl is white as a ghost, first Susan's husband and now another had followed. Derek could tell she holds fear within, so he kneels down and gives her an embrace. Trying to find words, the father speaks to his daughter.

"I know what you heard kind of shocks you, hell, it gives me a bit of a scare. Listen, just forget about it, I am sure the police will handle this maniac. Anyway, you need to try and get up and ready for school.." Derek says soothingly.

Josie climbs up on the couch and snuggles in, hugging a nearby pillow, dreading the idea of getting ready for school. Derek finds his car keys and goes back in the bedroom. After giving his wife a peck on the lips, the man heads on out to his car and is off to work, late.

Trench does not have it's own hospital, so Andrea is taking to Spontania General, Spontania is a fairly larger city off the border of Trench, but still within Georgia state lines. Larry Bora has long since left for home. Mark and Patricia Salem now join their daughter Andrea in her room. They have recently told the police she would have to answer questions at a later date. As for Seth Wake, he has stepped outside, not wanting to deal with the cops himself. The hospital sits on a river, Seth looks out over the water, taking in the view. He removes a cigarette from his breast pocket and packs it against his lighter. Then, placing it between his lips, Wake lights the tobacco inhaling slightly. Out on the river a water skier glides skillfully across the water. Seth puffs on his cigarette, thoughts of earlier events dance in his head. A slight grin comes to his face as he starts back to the front of the building. Minutes later, Wake finishes up his smoke and drops it on the ground, extinguishing it with his foot. Returning inside, he finds the nearest elevator and proceeds to the third floor, where Andrea rests soundly.

Back at the Lastings house, Josie finishes up getting ready for school, even though she is already late. Jennifer wakes Brad so she can give her daughter a ride. Naturally the young boy tests her patience, he squeals as she carries him into the dining room.

"I don't wanna go bye-bye," the lad screams.

Josie rolls her eyes, her little brothers acts quickly become tiring. After what seems to be an eternity, Jennifer, Josie, and little Brad exit the house going towards the mini-van parked only yards away. Off in the distance Josie's eyes find two men watching them. The cold hand of fear wraps its chilling fingers around her, Ash glares upon catching the girl's eye, Ambrose stands near.

"Mom, there's, there's two guys watching us, look right over there." Josie whispers, not wanting the onlookers to know she is speaking.

Jennifer looks to the spot in which her daughter had focused, now nothing can be seen. "You probably just imagined it, I mean the news this morning and your friend at work. Your mind is just a little paranoid, that's all dear." explains her mother.

Josie shakes her head convinced otherwise, she knows they were standing right behind the bushes across the street. Fortunately now it is only a picture of green grass and lush plant life. Upon entering the vehicle, Jennifer Lastings carefully backs from the drive. Reaching the main road, the mini-van shifts into drive and takes off down the street.

Only a few houses down, Larry Bora awakes with a feeling of loneliness. Apparently his wife has already gotten up, maybe to get an early start on some yard work. That had been the couple's big thing for quite some time now. The grass never got too tall, and the gardens always looked fresh and watered. Pretty flowers line the walk to the house and greenery compliment the porch. Sassing up the lawn had been what you would call their hobby for years. Larry looks out the blinds and finds no one. The elder man's clouded vision prevents him from seeing drops of blood spotted across the rug. Slowly but surely, Bora walks through his house attempting to locate his wife. A creaking of the floor echoing from the din brings the man in that direction. Delores Bora lay soundly on the couch, a colorful afghan covers her to the shoulders. Larry quietly walks over to her, then leans down to give a kiss on the cheek. The man's eyes blink several times, then he takes a closer look at his loves neck. Blood runs down over her shoulder and a chunk of skin is missing from her neck. Upon seeing this horrible sight, Larry begins to wheeze, pain shoots through his chest, then to his shoulder and arm. The room spins around. Pictures of his children and grandchildren stick in his mind. They are spread out evenly over the walls. His kids are watching him, watching him die, the eyes on the wall stare right at him. Only moments later, Larry Bora falls to the floor, clasping his shoulder and chest. Ash walks in from the shadows, evil flashes all over the man. The same knife that took Robert Falls' life is clenched in his hand. Now we get a better look at it. The handle is a beige color with a serpent etched red into it. The stainless steel blade extends about four inches and looks to be sharp as a razor. Ash kneels to the floor sticking the knife into Bora's side, then removes it. The shiny blade now covered in blood is raised to the Gothic figures mouth. He runs his tongue from the handle to the point of the knife. From behind Ambrose speaks.

"Still the search continues, he's not the one we need."

Ash returns to his feet, sheathing his knife. "You could be wrong... but your not. Remember, Abraham explained it could be any one, young or old."

Ambrose agrees and the two exit the scene, leaving two more dead. As they leave, Ash locks the door behind them, then moves on.

Michael Lastings struggles his way up the ladder as him and his buddy Timothy Smilot grapple with a walk board. They lay either end on that of roof jacks then catch their breath before climbing back down. It's a two story climb from the ground to the top of the latter, quite a hull when lugging a walk board along with you. Kenny Marks and Dale Sanders also work with the guys. The boss, Eric Mays, has taking a personal day, likely to get some things done at home. Eric usually works right along with the crew, today happens to be a rare. The roof Michael Lastings and the rest of the guys have been sent to do is rather large, not to mention steep. Timmy sizes up the bundle before him, then brings one up over his shoulder, Michael does the same. Again the long journey up the rungs pursues. Once enough shingles have been toted, the gang will be able to get a good start on this particular side of the house. Kenny and Dale currently are finishing off a few rows just over the peak.

Talking as they work, Timothy speaks over his shoulder to Michael. "Did you here about Steven Mass, he had a pretty crazy run in with Eugene Browder's killer? I heard that he tried to shoot the man, but he just got right back up."

"Pretty damn scary if you ask me, not to mention it is the same son of a bitch that crossed paths with us at the ball court. Man, it could be one of us dead."

Timothy has no real reply to this, he quickly changes the subject. "So Josie has the hots for my little brother huh? Damn, I have to admit, she is a hotty." Smilot laughs after commenting on Michael's sister.

"Watch it now. Cause if I end up throwing you off the roof, I sure as hell am not going to dig you up when you sink ten feet into that clay like shit below. Besides, I think it is your brother who has the hots for MY sister, ha!

Dale pops his head up over the peak to join the conversation. "Sorry Mike, I have to agree with Smiley, your sister is hotter than fresh laid Georgia asphalt. Looks like you might be outnumbered Mikey boy." Dale liked to tease the other guys with their names, just kind of his nature, Smiley instead of Smilot, or Mikey boy in place of Michael, you get the picture.

Kenny Marks chimes in, "You guys are trying to piss the man off aren't you. I mean I would never talk that way about ol Michael's sister. After all, his mother is much hotter." Everyone laughs except Mike, he scrunches his face up and shakes his head.

"You guys are real comedians, you know that. Real fucking funny!" All four now have a small laugh, this including Michael of course. Next they continue nailing shingles only to stop again moments later. Off in the distance, some wolves howl simultaneously. Nothing is said, seconds later, the shingle laying continues.

The school bell rings at Trench High to signal the end of first period classes. Speakers are spread throughout the school so the ringing is quite loud. The school itself is built of white blocks, dark blue paint outline the windows. Across the front lay two large patches of Astor-turf looking grass. The center doors lead to the office and a canopy covers most of the walkways. Josie Lastings gathers her books and quickly makes her way into the hallway, which is already full with students. Craig Johnson would soon be exiting his Government class only a few rooms down. She loves to follow him to his locker, and then upstairs to his second period class. It never seems to leave her much time to get where she needs to be herself, though she does not mind at all. Soon her crush comes into sight, strutting his way out of the doorway the same as he always does. What a cute little strut it is, she thinks to herself. For a moment her thoughts go back to the daydream she had, and suddenly she feels hot all over. Josie quickly takes chase only to bump into James Smilot, who she had danced with at the Autumn Dance.

"Hey Josie, if your in a big hurry, its cool. I was just curios about, maybe, I mean... You want to go out." James finally blurts out. The girl says nothing, peering over his shoulder as Craig slowly fades out of sight.

"Huh, what did you say?"

James turns around and sees what has her attention. "Don't tell me, you're hooked too. I don't get what all you girls see in him. He's a jerk. He thinks jocks rule the world or something. Maybe someday I will put him in his place."

Josie turns back to James, "Oh him, he doesn't impress me much. But he was wearing this really cool shirt." The girl smiles big as this thought runs through her mind. "No he don't impress me much, just enough to make me all hot and bothered under my skirt and want to explode."

"Oh well, anywise. I was wandering if you would like to go out or something?" Smilot asks again.

Ms. Lastings smiles, "Well, it sounds good to me. Where would you like to go, maybe a movie?"

"Great", he answers. So I will call you tonight and we will set a good time."

Josie agrees and the two walk on to their next class. Josie pouts to herself a bit for missing Craig Johnson, then forgets about it. Lisa Mays has second period with Josie, and for the first time they both get to class a couple minutes early and have time to sit and converse.. Soon the bell rings out again to start class.

Out beyond city limits, Andrea lays awake in her hospital bed. Seth Wake stands at the foot of her bed and her parents sit on opposite sides. Mark Salem has not yet been told of his best friends death. They had not turned on the news, or left the hospital for any period of time, or perhaps they might have known. Not to mention, his daughter missing had kept his mind on one thing and one thing only, her.

"Seth, we would like to thank you again for watching over our daughter, I do not know how you did it, but you kept her alive and as safe as possible." Mark says appreciatively.

Seth stands with most of his weight on his right leg and his arms crossed. His eyes look full of wonder, beautiful, but incredibly dark. "Well, Mr. and Mrs. Salem, I did what I had to do for this particular situation, nothing more, nothing less."

Andrea struggles to sit up, an IV has been put in her right arm, she is careful not to pull it. "I heard Seth yell a little and then all went quiet, I almost passed out when the first beast landed on the hood. Then one of the wolves snarled from the side I think. Finally the wolf on the hood broke the windshield, soon after that all went black. When I awoke, Seth came walking up and the wolves were gone. And apparently he had carried me a couple miles to be sure I was safe."

"Just did what I felt I had to, Seth starts, but now I need to be moving on, I have other dragons to slay. Not to mention my parents are most likely worried sick. So, see you later Andrea." Wake nods to her bows his head slightly to the Salem's then exits the hospital room. Along the wall there is ugly greenish wallpaper. The young man walks on until he reaches the stairs. Seth lights another cigarette on the few flights down, disregarding all smoking regulations. As he comes out on the lobby floor, a nurse scolds him and urges him to extinguish his tobacco. The lady in white watches as the disrespectful boy before her drops the stogie to the floor and crushes it with his boot. Next he gives her an irresistible smile and leaves through the doorway marked exit. Upon entering the air outside, Seth Wake stops for a moment and speaks to no one but himself. "The time is near." is all he says, and mysteriously disappears.

Chapter 11

THE SUN SHINES AT its peak down on Spontania General Hospital. A patrol car marked Trench police finds its way into a emergency vehicles only spot right near the front doors and two officers dressed in their blues step out. The cops had grown weary of waiting for answers, so many deaths, in so little time. The two men on duty want details of Andrea's attack, wild animals, or masked murderer. They had to find out any clue they could to see if this linked to the murders. The policemen wait impatiently as the elevator makes it's upward decent. Soon they find Andrea's room, her parents sit with the young girl as the questions are asked. The first officer begins. "Now, if you could tell us again, how you got from the school dance to the location in which the Chevrolet Blazer was found?"

Andrea is tired and obviously does not feel like talking, but does. "I told you earlier, Seth and myself went for a ride. We turned down a dirt road and became stuck in the mud. Before I knew what was happening, these wild beasts attacked the vehicle. Somehow, Seth managed to fight them off."

The second officer started in, "OK., are you sure it was a pair of wolves, I mean could it have been possible a human was involved?"

"It was wolves, two or three of them, I seen them with my own eyes, growling and snapping. Wolves attacked us not humans. And he got rid of them, and when I awoke they were gone. From that point Seth flagged down a ride and got me here for some help."

"Just trying to put it all together ma'am, now could you tell us the color of the animals. Try to be specific." stated officer one.

Andrea became very frustrated, "No, I can't tell you what color they were, it is not exactly the first thing that came to mind. You know, oh look at the pretty wolves getting ready to rip me apart. How pretty its brown mixes with the black. What are you going to arrest them?"

Officer one rolls his eyes, "Listen, this is important, we had a little trouble with a white wolf, no markings, only hours ago. Can you try and remember?"

Andrea says nothing for a couple minutes, the cops can tell she is concentrating. Her hands move to rub her eyes and then the girl grunts as she sits up even straighter. "I think that there was a white one, I am not sure if it had any markings or not, though I am pretty sure it was white. It was very dark and I had been half scared out of my mind, so I hope you can understand why I did not get a good look."

The second officer clears his throat and upon writing a couple more notes in his little book, he speaks. "We understand, and do appreciate all you are doing. As my partner had said, we may be able to link your white wolf with the one we had a run in with. And as strange as it may sound, the wolf may be related with the murders that have occurred. Let me explain what I mean. We received a call that a break in was in progress. As we arrived on the scene, one of our officers had already taking chase. The man fled into the woods, and as we attempted to apprehend him, a white wolf appeared out of no where causing us to lose the suspect."

Mr. Salem scratches his head and looks to the officers.

"That seems strange enough, but I seriously doubt the two wolves were the same. I mean that sounds just a little crazy to me, if you know what I mean."

"Yes it does, and it has made us wonder exactly what we are really up against. Anyway, we have kept your daughter from her rest long enough. So if my partner has nothing more, we appreciate your time."

Officer one nods his head and the two strong arms of the law exit stage right. Only, a few moments later, officer one comes back in.

"I apologize, but there is just one more thing." He pauses for a moment, opening his small notebook and skims through it then speaks again. "The first time we came, we got a name and a short explanation of what had happened to you. I have the name Seth Wake here, and I wonder, are you sure that is the correct name?"

Andrea Salem speaks right up, "Yes, that is correct. Why do you ask, has he been in some trouble?"

"No," the boy in blue starts, "It is just, we looked him up in our computers, scanned for his name half a dozen times. And the strange thing is, he is no where to be found."

The final school bell rings as one more school day comes to an end. Josie and Lisa run out the buildings side exits racing to get to Jennifer Lastings van first. Behind them, a little distant, they can hear a teacher telling them to slow down, they pay her no mind. Jennifer asks how their day was, and of course the girls reply, "Lame." Lisa could hardly wait to get over Tommy's house, he would be feeling better now and be able to go out and do some things.

"So anything new girls, or same old school education." Jennifer turns the van over and the engine cranks to life. After letting another vehicle pass, the woman pulls away from the curb.

"Eh, well, we were giving a stupid report to do. Something about the history of our city." Josie answers with an unenthusiastic voice. Jennifer knows she hates reports.

"Yeah, Lisa adds, you know. We have to look up some of the great events that helped shape our city. Important people, important happenings, in other words, research paper."

Jennifer kind of laughs at the girl's comments. "I will help how ever I can, and you better not wait till the last minute this time Josie. You girls let me know if there is anything I can do to help. Maybe pick something up, or if you need a ride anywhere I will be glad to take you."

The two young women nod and the minivan takes a right onto Lisa's street. Her house is unaccompanied by any others, it sits in the middle of an open field. Maybe about five acres, a long driveway extends out from the building. Once arriving home, it is probable Lisa will have her mother take her over her boyfriend, Tommy's house.

Josie pulls the van door shut and watches on as her mom shifts from neutral into drive. Then, with a pitiful look on her face, she asks.

"Mom, do you think I could drive home, I mean it has been weeks since I have had the chance?"

Jennifer touches her foot to the brake and the vehicle comes to a stop. "I think that might be all right Josie, but I warn you. If you start driving this the same way your father caught you driving Michael's car, you're in for it."

Josie kind of sinks back in the chair, feeling a little ashamed. You see, about a month prior to this, Josie stayed the night over her brother's house. Michael decided to let her drive, since she did have her learner's permit and he happened to be over eighteen. So, she decided to get a case of led foot and found herself doing seventy miles an hour down one of the many country back roads. By chance, they met up with Derek coming the other direction. First the two youngings had no idea good old dad had any idea how fast they were going. Later they found his estimated guess would prove better than they thought.

So Jennifer climbs out of the passenger seat to let Josie drive, she makes sure to do the speed limit all the way home.

Chapter 12

Derek Lastings wipes the sweat from his brow as he spies the clock on the wall. Almost going home time, he thinks to himself. Then, from the loud speaker hanging some twenty feet up, an announcement booms through the factory, echoing the walls.

"Delivery at receiving, all technicians report. Delivery at receiving, all technicians report."

Derek kind of shakes his head in dismay, then follows the concrete floor to shipping and receiving. Three bay doors line the back wall, one roll door has been opened, parked tight against the wall is the delivery truck. Most deliveries consisted of twelve to fifteen pallets, all had to be pulled off the trailer, and sorted by that of color and company. With all the techs working at the load, it doesn't take too incredibly long. Once finished, Derek punches the time clock and ends yet another intricate day.

He leaves the factory and climbs into his old pickup. It smokes horribly upon starting. Once a fellow employee pointed this out to Lastings, he replied with a laugh. "Don't worry about it, she is plenty old enough." Both men had their chuckle. On the way home Derek decides to stop in for a few groceries, after all, Trench's lone grocery store would be on the way. As he drives on, the man gathers a few things in his head to pick up. The parking lot, as usual, is nearly empty. Derek hops out of his pickup and makes his way in. On the way through the door, a young man resting against the front of the building glares at him, Lastings ignores it. Seth Wake smiles at this as he watches the man before him enter the grocer. After a few minutes, the father of three exits the building again, this time carrying two paper bags. Suddenly he runs into someone, almost dropping his groceries. "Excuse me, a voice calls.

"So sorry Derek calls back. As the guy walks on, Lastings takes notice it is the same character who had glared at him on the way in. Again he thinks nothing of it, sitting the groceries down in the bed of his truck. Strangely, a drop of blood trickles down his arm, almost as if something small had punctured it. Quickly, Derek Lastings survey the area, searching for the boy who he had run into. No one in sight though, Wake had already ducked out. Derek now simply blots his arm with a napkin and gets in the truck. Seconds later he is speeding homeward.

As for Seth, he tucks an unlit cigarette behind his ear and peers at the blood-covered needle held neatly in his fingertips.

"Not much, but tis enough." Seth's words are low and mysterious. Now he touches the bloody metallic object to his lips, tasting the touch of blood that blankets it. "No Derek Lastings, you aren't worth the struggle." He then drops the needle to the ground and removes the stogy from his ear. As he places it in his mouth, Wake touches the unlit end with the tip of his finger. Now the tobacco begins to smolder, and smoke. Next Seth inhales deeply and now the cigarette is lit completely. As the young man blows smoke from his nose, he turns to the back of the store and then disappears into the trees.

"Eugene Browder was killed, when, who, what do you mean?" Mark Salem could not believe his ears, his best friend had been murdered. His wife Sandra hugs his neck, a nurse had dispersed the news to her and she had no choice but to tell her husband.

"I don't know, all I know is he is gone, and someone took him from us. I am so sorry honey." Sandra speaks grievingly, tears begin to well up in her eyes. Mark does not say anything else, he merely turns back to his daughters room and goes to her bedside. Andrea would be able to leave in a few hours. The girl had improved considerably and the doctors felt she no longer needed to be there. Andrea still lay in bed, trying to determine what the cop meant. "Well, we put his name through the computer half a dozen times, and strangely enough, we found him no where." The words uttered again and again in her head, almost like a record when it skips and plays the same thing over and over again.

"Hey, are you still with us doll." Mark calls to his daughter, trying to hide the pain in his voice.

"Yeah dad, I am still trying to make sense of things, I mean why would Seth give me a fake name or lie to me at all for that matter?"

"I don't know dear, people can be awkward sometimes. But a, you know, Eugene has run into a little trouble darling. It seems someone entered his house with him unaware, and well, Eugene is pretty bad off honey." Mark himself now began to feel the tears in his eyes, he did his best to fight them back, and somehow succeeded. "Eugene has been, has been killed Andrea." Somehow Mark Salem found the words, and it was not easy, not easy at all.

Poor Andrea felt overwhelmed, Eugene Browder had always been like an uncle to her. The girl sinks back in her hospital bed and closes her eyes. She remembers the times Eugene had taking her to the river with him. He had even bought her, her own fishing rod, it seemed to be such a short time ago. She could also remember how she hated bating the hooks because she did not want to get slimy. Most of the time Browder had to do it for her, although sometimes Andrea got brave and gave it a try herself. On rare occasion though.

The family comforted one another, life seemed to be going pretty rough on them. Unfortunately, it would only get worse.

We now turn back to Michael Lastings, he too is now getting off work. He loads the last ladder on the truck and then ties it off. After recording the time, quarter till four, Mike waves bye to the rest of the crew and drives off. He comes to the end of the drive and something catches his eye. Right there next to him on the passenger seat are near a dozen razor sharp teeth. They stand up, points down, punctured into the cloth of the seat. And though Michael can not make out what it means or stands for, they seem to lay in a pattern. This is how it appears.

ΛΛΛΛΛ

ΛΛΛ

ΛΛΛΛΛ

What could it possibly mean, he's not sure, and maybe it is better he doesn't. Michael covers them with his coat and squeals tires out of the drive. It would take about twenty minutes to get from his current location to the shop, there he would drop off the work truck and pick up his own vehicle. Something very strange was sweeping over the city of Trench, Michael Lastings had to find out what. Soon the young man reaches his destination, he parks the truck, and drops the keys under the mat of the shop door. Michael goes to his Mustang and retrieves an extra shirt from with in. After plucking each jagged tooth from its spot in the seat, he wraps them in his shirt tightly. Carefully he lays the bundle on the passenger seat of his old Ford and pulls away. The gas tank needle rests on the E mark, just my damn luck Michael thinks to himself. A bit ahead on the right, an old Exxon sat off the shoulder of the road, here he would fill the tank, then set off to the police station.

Down at the county jail, Barry Spencer comes walking from within, he has his typical bad ass strut going on and a look on his face that says, "I'm all that and more baby." Across the lot, Kevin Riley and Larry Stant wait for him next to Riley's car. It's an older make of Dodge, and looks to be a little hot under the hood. From a distance, Seth Wake looks on, a grim look is on his face and his skin seems to be a light gray. His eyes blacken as he stares down at the three boys at the bottom of the hill across the parking lot. The guys pile into the old Charger and dust flies as they leave the scene. Now a grin replaces the evil expression on Wake's face, and once again he disappears into the shadows.

Chapter 13

JOSIE LASTINGS SITS AT the dining room table trying to finish up the last of her homework. Her father had arrived home by this time and already started one of his many projects, he often left work only to come home and work about on other tasks. Jennifer Lastings walks in from the kitchen, she had recently finished up on a couple dishes and now had other plans to tend to.

"Josie, would you mind watching Brad for a little while, I need to run to the grocery store and pickup a few things."

"Mom, dad picked some groceries up on the way home, what else do we need?"

"Well, Jennifer began, "You know your father. He only picks up the things he thinks we need, none of which consists of cereal for in the morning or bath tissue."

Josie laughs, "All right mom, I will watch him, I can only hope he will be somewhat congenial. But don't worry, I wont get my hopes up, or hold my breath for that matter. By the way, where is the little brat."

As if he had been cued to do so, Bradford runs in from the back hallway, he is soaked. He light blue shirt has turned dark, and his shorts look as if he has wet himself. (Yes, he is potty trained by the way) Jennifer and Josie stare at him, thinking they know exactly where he came from.

"You haven't been in the fish tank, cause we have been right here and you weren't. So, I guess a little boy has been playing in the toilet again." Jennifer proclaims.

The boy has a poutty look on his face, and he looks at his mother and yells, "Nah-uh."

Josie decides she will take care of the mess, and she walks her mom to the door. Then she turns to her adoring little brother and grabs him by the hand, leading him in to change his clothes and dry off. Josie knew for sure that Brad would turn into more of a choir than doing her homework had been. And it was not five minutes after drying him off, the boy took one of his toy blocks and threw it across the room. This made him laugh hysterically, then he would pick up another and throw it. The first one simply flew through the air and landed on the carpet, the second however smacked into a lamp almost knocking it to the floor.

"Bradford Lee, you better quit that before I stick you in a corner, and believe me you won't get out until mom gets home."

Brad only sticks his tongue out and spits at her, taunting his sister. Josie gets up to chase after him as he darts in the other direction. Abruptly the phone rings, putting a cease on the chase momentarily. After a third ring, Josie picks up the receiver, "Hello?"

"Yeah, is, um, Josie there?" The voice on the other end was clearly that of James Smilot, Josie decided she would have a little fun with him."

"No, Josie had a date tonight with Craig Johnson. She said to tell Jamie, if he calls, that she would get back to him."

Silence can be heard on the other end of the phone, until Josie finally begins to laugh. James realizes he has been duped and speaks up. "OK, that was cute, yeah, I could have done with out the Craig Johnson part, but cute none the less. The conversation went on for a bit, though not as long as the one the morning before, then they decided they would see a seven o'clock movie and got of the phone. Now Josie continues the on going fight with her little brother.

Michael Lastings pulls up the parking break of his car and steps out. He has arrived at the Trench Sheriffs office. He gathers the teeth once again and begins to walk briskly to the building before him. The sheriff's office looks like one you might see in an old western. To either side of the parking lot are trees and more trees. They sometimes made it difficult to find the place. After passing through a metal detector, Michael enters the office marked sheriff above the door. A man of medium height with gray hair and a lisp on his top lip stands behind a brown counter. The officer smiles revealing his missing teeth, Michael explains his situation and shows the officer the teeth. The cop takes them and walks through a quaint doorway in the back of the office and disappears. Minutes later, after discussing it with the other boys in blue, the man returns.

"Son, after conversing with the others, I have come to the conclusion that, that is, these are wolves teeth. As for how they got into your work truck, or what that there symbol you explained to me means, well son, it is beyond me."

"I understand officer, I think I know now where they came from though. He is trying to play mind games, well, he'll get his."

Lastings thanks the officer for his time and walks briskly back out to his vehicle. Now outside, Michael finds Seth Wake standing between him and his car. He stands arms folded, leaning against young Lastings car door. Yes of course, a cigarette hangs from the corner of his mouth and a dark glare is on his face. Mike keeps his distance, giving the impression that it is OK if this stranger props himself up on his personal property.

"Good afternoon Michael, or do you prefer MR. Lastings?"

Michael swallows the lump in his throat and goose bumps run up both arms. Somehow this guy knew Michael's name, and they had never met one another. That wasn't all either, something was in the air. A feeling of darkness, a feeling of evil. Mike almost wants to run, leave and get away from the being before him. Though, he does not, he stays and watches on. Wake steps away from the Mustang, his window is no longer rolled up as he left it, now it is gaping open. Still Lastings does not say a word, Seth looks at him in amusement.

"I thought I would let your car air out, hope you don't mind."

With one final puff, Wake shows Michael the lit cigarette, then carelessly tosses it through the open car window. "What the hell are you doing?" Michael yells at Seth as he almost dives into the car searching for the lit tobacco. It lay right under the front of the driver seat. Michael grabs it and snuffs it out in his ashtray. Furious, the boy leaps from his car to take after Seth, only Seth is nowhere to be found. Angry and confused, Michael Lastings returns to his Ford Mustang and speeds off.

While Mike races around the city in his car, his mother chats on the phone with her old high school friend Toni Hailey.

"So what have you been up to?"

"Well, I had to pick some things up from the grocery store that Derek forgot, I had just arrived home when you called. I tell you, he can be so funny some times. I mean, he could write the grocery list before he left and still he would come home missing something."

"Yeah, but if you remember, he didn't have the best memory in high school either. Like that day it was the anniversary of the day he asked you out. You were so upset because you had asked him what today was. And he says Tuesday." She laughs and Jennifer soon joins her.

Indeed the two did have their share of arguments in high school, but Derek always seemed to find a way to melt his way back into her heart. In his senior year, the young Derek Lastings had been seeing his future wife for almost two years. This is the time he made what he still considers the biggest mistake of his life.

Jennifer stayed two classes longer than Derek in the twelfth grade and Lastings always showed back up at school to pick her up. He would be standing up against his old pickup waiting when the bell rang. Then greet her once seeing her exit the building. Another young lady by the name of Allison Tate, a tall blond with legs to kill for and large chest to boot, began speaking to him on occasion. This went on for a bit, then one day Derek brought a puppy along with him in which he had recently adopted from the pound. Allison came out when the bell first rang, it usually took Jennifer a few minutes. The young woman stopped to see the cute little animal and did her best to show off her cleavage while doing so. Lastings could not help but stare at her wondrous breasts. Things like this went on for a bit, Allison of course making tracks before Jenny came out. Derek slowly became interested and began to notice more and more the sexual arousement he felt when Tate hung around. So he secretly began to flirt back and from there they started joking about sneaking around. The next thing you know they were in bed together and Derek was screwing her brains out.

Needless to say, his girlfriend soon found out, as they always do. Jennifer went off the deep end. She returned everything he ever gave her and ended the relationship. Lasting ended his fling with Allison Tate as well, in hopes that his true love would forgive. It would not be right away, though after several dozen roses and many apologies later, Jennifer Valley took him back. On they're third night back together, the two made love time and time again. A baby had been conceived and due to this sudden occurrence, Jennifer Valley soon became Jennifer Lastings. Unfortunately, the baby would not make it to the second trimester, she lost it. The miscarriage broke both the young adults hearts. They grew closer through the whole ordeal miraculously, for they turned to one another to help make it through. And a couple years later, Mr. and Mrs. Lastings would have a wonderful baby boy. They would name him Michael, and from there, as we know, two more would follow.

Jennifer switches the phone from one ear to the other and the two women talk only a few minutes longer before hanging up. Upon hearing the dial tone, the mother of three pauses a moment thinking again of the one she lost, then pushes the thought aside.

On the other side of the phone line, Toni Haley has already hung up the phone. She had rather enjoyed talking to her old High School buddy about past memories. Now, Toni for the first time realizes she is not alone. She breaks into a cold sweat as she turns and finds Ash staring a hole right through her. Haley tries to scream but the sound does not come. Ash reaches out with lightning quick hands and grabs the woman by the neck, long sharp fingernails pierce the skin. Now the sound comes, now Toni screams, now she shrieks over and over as the blood begins to spew from the holes in her neck. His fingernails are like blades and dig deeper yet into Haley's throat. And soon, it grows silent!

Chapter 14

ONCE AGAIN NIGHT HAS come and gone and a new day dawns. Josie Lastings had enjoyed her date with James the night before. The movie they had seen turned out to be really good and she even got a chance to see Craig Johnson passing through in the mall. Now Josie stands between two long bookshelves holding a book in her hand. She slowly thumbs through it, trying to find anything of interest. Within the book is copies of old newspapers and important documents in which helped shape the city of Trench. The papers dated back to the 1960's and 70's. She wanted something more, so she picked through a couple more books before one caught her eye. Before Trench City was printed on the cover. Inside, she found many legends and facts of the city. Josie cringed as she read over a few of the articles. One told how a mother crashed and burned after swerving off the road to avoid an oncoming truck. They say you can see the boy walking down old Turnbuckle Lane on certain dark nights. Another spoke of The Demons of the Lake, which were supposedly people with no eyes who had been damned and cursed to live eternity at the bottom of Trouble Lake. Legend had it that the demons would only surface when the voice of a child could be heard. It was all very interesting to her, the girl flipped a couple more pages and found a picture that made her feel very uneasy. Several people lay dead, making up what looked to be some kind of symbol. Above the picture reads this.

> *The witch Alise laid many to rest, here is a portion of her victims!*

Pretty weird, she thinks, as she turns the page. What she finds next seems even stranger than the picture, maybe even more frightening.

> *Aloise Wake was finally stopped and killed by Joseph Critton. Unfortunately, it ended in death for both, but not before Wake had taken the lives of eleven others. She was believed to be a witch of great power , mixed with the likes of the common vampire.*

Josie quit reading for a moment, took a deep breath, and as she read on...

> *Autopsy reports gave reason to believe that Alise Wake had given birth prior to death. Location of the offspring is to this day, unknown.*

This is where the young girl slammed the book shut and spoke into the air.

"She couldn't be related!"

Without out another seconds thought, young Josie Lastings takes the book to the counter and checks it out. This is almost her last period of the day, and she can not wait to go home.

Elsewhere, Larry Stant and his buddies are up to their old tricks again. The three were supposed to be in school hours ago, not that they gave a damn. As they turn out they're pockets, each brag about the stolen items within. Barry Spencer walks on ahead, the other two follow closely. Up ahead they spot Seth leaning up against a building. He appears to be alone, and his back faces them.

"Hey, Barry whispers, aint that the guy from the dance, said some shit about the strong and the weak."

Kevin Riley squints his eyes, "Sure enough is!"

"Well, let me say this, no one talks shit to me, Barry Spencer, and gets away with it. I'll show him who the hell the strong is!"

Planning on teaching Seth a lesson, the boys sneak quietly up behind him until they are only feet away.

"I don't suggest doing that, that is, if you know what is good for you." Wake does not turn around, his words are cold and confident.

"Go to hell." Barry Spencer charges the man with his back to them. Seth spins around in a flash, grabbing the boy's throat and slamming him into the concrete wall. All the air in his body shoots out at once, Spencer slides down the bricks to the ground, doing his best to catch his breath.

"OK, you think you're a tough son of a bitch huh, well lets see." Kevin Riley picks up a branch that lay near and starts towards Seth. Larry Stant pulls a switchblade from his boot and joins his friend's side. Riley swings the branch like a baseball bat and connects with the target. The wood breaks and splinters over Seth Wakes head and face. The man falls to his knee for a mere moment, then returns to his feet. His eyes now hold no color, only blackness. A couple spots of blood run from Wakes forehead, but the dark figure grins anyway. Then, with the simple wave of a hand, Kevin Riley becomes air born, his arms flailing. He lands with a sickening crunch up against a large tree. Larry Stant stands in shock for a moment, then regains his composure. He strikes Seth directly in the gut, his switchblade becomes buried in the man's stomach. Pain shoots though Wake's entire body, only to look at him, it seems he has felt nothing. Seth brings his arm back and then thrusts it forward. His hand slices into Stant's neck like a sharp blade, blood spews onto Wakes hand and arm then joins his own as it falls to the ground below.

"The strong always prey on the weak, especially when they outnumber the other. Fortunately Larry, the weak was indeed the strong. And , well, the strong proved simply, not strong enough!"

Seth's eyes now return to normal as he let's the body fall and turns to walk away. He leaves two dead, and one fallen. Barry Spencer lay still trying to catch his breath, and after watching his friends get killed with such ease, he does not want to get up.

Slowly but surely, the city of Trench is turning into a state of emergency. A total of six now lay dead, the police are at a loss. The residents of Trench are becoming frightened to even live their own lives. Jennifer Lastings sits at home by herself, with the exception of her son Brad. Reports of Larry and Delores Bora have really hit home. Jennifer's friend Toni has not yet been found, only more grief for the Lastings lying in wait. Currently Josie would be meeting with Tommy and Lisa for a ride home. The girl makes sure to show her friends what she had read in the book. Tommy is bewildered at the similarity in his and Joseph Critton's name. He thinks he will ask his sister if she thinks Joseph could be any relation. As for Seth and Alise, Tommy nor Lisa knew what to think of that either.

"So you don't think the two of you are related in any way." Josie waits impatiently for an answer, the whole situation intrigues her. Tommy looks up from the ground.

"No, I don't. And like I said, my sister might know better, though, I doubt it." Besides, it isn't that big of a deal. Even if this Seth Wake you met is related to Alice, or Alise, it has nothing to do with me here and now."

Worriedly, Lisa puts her two cents in. "I thought the guy was awfully strange myself, I mean, where did he come from? Tommy, you have already been hurt once, I can't handle it again."

Shaking his head, "You two girls are making entirely too much out of this. I know with all that is going on you girls are frightened, hell I'm a little scared myself. We just need to concentrate on school, and work. Try and forget everything else, even if it's just for a minute."

Josie rubs her eyes, "That may be easy for you to do Tommy, but I had a co.-worker murdered, and the Bora's live just down the street from me. And you expect me to forget all that."

Tommy starts to reply and then stops short as Lisa's parents pull up. All three students get in and the van slowly pulls off. On the way home, Josie points out the Salem family coming the other way, Andrea included, they wave at each other. Soon the van is at the Lastings house.

As she gets out of the van, Josie notices her brother's car in the drive. The Mays no more and drove off, and Steven Mass along with Matthew Turry arrive. Michael had given them a phone call to meet him at his parent's house. The small group of young adults talk for a bit, then they all go on inside. Michael shows the wolves teeth to all and then explains how he had come across them.

"That's weird Michael, but we have some bad news hon." Jennifer does her best to hold back the tears as she explains what happened to Larry and Delores Bora. Everyone keeps silent when she is done, Michael shakes his head. He feels terrible about the whole situation. Josie breaks the silence after a couple long minutes go by, she brings their attention to the book, Before Trench City. As she opens to the pages discussing Alise Wake, Michael grabs the book from her hand.

"Where did you get this?" Michael is almost yelling at his sister as he stares at the picture in front of him.

"At the library, what is your problem?" Josie has been taking by surprise from her brother's actions, she does not know what to think. There would be no immediate response, only silence as the man looks from the page of the book to the teeth and back again. Matthew Turry stands behind his friend trying to peek over his shoulder at the pages of the book.

"The positions of these people, the positions of these eleven corpses are exactly that of how I found the wolves teeth." Michael can't believe his eyes, what in the hell does it all mean.

"That's crazy, but there is something else, the name of the woman who slaughtered those poor souls is Alise Wake. Wake, does that sound familiar?"

Jennifer Lastings interrupts her daughter, "Lets not jump to conclusions. I am sure it means absolutely nothing. A lot of crazy things are going on and nobody really knows why. We cant just go making things up though."

Michael argues, he sets the book down on the table then looks to his mother. "Look, it says here that Alise Wake was a vampire witch. The guy I seen at the ball court was a damn vampire. He showed me his fangs, his eyes were black, that's not human. I am not making this up, I mean, I even had a nightmare about this guy."

Steven Mass starts to say his piece then thinks better of it. Josie starts in again, "I bet you saw Seth, he is exactly like the woman."

"Stop it," Jennifer yells, "your all talking crazy. Now we need to drop this whole thing and change the subject." All is quiet. The sound of a vehicle pulling into the drive comes from outside. Derek Lastings steps from his truck, fatigue had definitely set in as the man had endured a hard days work. Slowly Derek makes his way up the walk and enters his home. Right away he can tell emotions are soaring. He says hello to the group then gives Jennifer a kiss hello. Then young Brad comes running out of the other room and runs straight for his dad.

"Daddy, daddy, your home"

Presently, at the home of the Salem's, Andrea and the rest of her family sit watching a movie Mark had rented earlier. Something about a killer asteroid headed for earth, there is at least a dozen movies to that effect. The doorbell rings interrupting the little get together and Andrea gets up to answer it. An injured Seth Wake stands on the other side, his hands and most of his clothes covered in blood. Andrea gasps at the sight of him.

"Oh my God, what happened to you?" The young girl wants to give Seth some support, but the sight of all that blood had froze her in her tracks.

Wake somehow continues to hold his own wait, almost as if the loss of his internal fluids had not even weakened him. "That is of no concern, I need blood so that I may regain my full strength. I am sorry Andrea, but I have to do what has to be done.!"

Andrea still does not move, Seth grabs her violently and pulls her to him, kissing her roughly. Moments later she falls limp to the porch's wooden floor. She is still alive, only out for the time being. Seconds later Mark Salem shows up at the door. The man finds his daughter passed out and immediately goes to her. He does not see her attacker waiting in the shadows. Now Seth takes a blade seemingly from out of thin air and grasps it with his right hand. The knife looks to be identical to Ash's. Seth moves forward and as Mr. Salem spins around, the knife became buried deep with in his windpipe. First Mark fights to catch a breath, then he yanks the knife from his throat and tosses it aside. Wake stands his ground, waiting for the man's next move. With one hand, Andrea's father holds his neck, and with the other he attempts to choke the dark being before him. Seth takes both his hands and put them on Marks shoulders. He forces him to his knees and now for the first time Seth Wake's razor sharp fangs are revealed. Mrs. Salem shows up right in time to see the flesh ripped from her husband's throat. The woman screams, then passes out from pure fright. The vampire has his feast with a good amount of Mark's blood before releasing his body and letting it crash to the porch. As for Mrs. Salem, there would be nothing she could do but to suffer the same fate. When finished, Seth has his full power back and his thirst well quenched. He stands over the two dead parents staring at the young girl before him. She would awake with in the hour. She would slowly begin to stir and the first bit of daylight would peak through the darkness. At first she will think she is in the woods again and the wolves have gone. Once to her feet though, Andrea will realize the awful truth of her surroundings. And then, a shriek will be heard for miles around as the girl yells again and again and again. She won't stop screaming until a passer by surveys the situation and forces the girl from the porch. The onlooker will shake her until she stops shrieking. Then Andrea will cry, she will cry until the tears dry up, asking why, over and over. But there will be no answer, no explanation. And finally, it will happen, that cloudiness will rush in and take any rational thought she has left. Her sight will become blurry and she will laugh hysterically. And yes, finally the young girl will lose any sanity she has left, for she would never be the same again.

Chapter 15

Tommy Critton and Lisa Mays sit on her parents couch snuggled up in a blanket together. The game show, Wheel of Fortune plays on the television set. Vanna flips over the last few letters of a catch phrase and both teenagers tell the other that they had known it all along. Lisa's mom stands in front of the counter in a small kitchen attempting to roll dough for cookies. Good ol' dad, as usual, has his head stuck up under the family vehicle. It had been time for an oil change for a month and he figured he should go ahead and take care of it. So Lisa and Tommy pretty much have the living room to themselves. The couple had already forgotten about the whole Joseph and Alise bit that they had talked about with Josie. The blanket they have around them covers them from the waist down and Lisa has already crept her hand over to her boyfriend's leg and began rubbing it. He has his arm around her neck and shoulders and uses it to pull her closer. She kisses him on the cheek and looks over her shoulder towards the kitchen. Apparently mom still has her hands full with the chocolate chip cookies. The young girl looks at Critton sensually and then slides her hand over between his legs and begins to unbutton his pants. Tommy closes his eyes as her fingers fall over their target. Her touch feels hot, immediately he becomes aroused. As Lisa closes her hand around him, the young man moved his arm from around her neck and quickly drops it under the covers and between his girl's legs. She moans quietly in his ear and again looks over her shoulder. Moments later, they are both being pleasured by the other ones skillful hand. It takes everything they have to keep quiet and stay under control.

They both jump when the phone rings from the in-table beside them. Both pull away in a flash and Lisa calls to her mom to let her know, "I got it." Tommy quickly re-buttons his pants being careful not to catch any thing and Lisa picks up the receiver.

"Hello," she calls as she tucks the phone between her shoulder and ear so she too could refasten herself before mom or dad arrives. Silence comes from the other end. "Hello!"

"You may see them by night, when the moon beams full over the valley, which shall smell of death." The voice on the other end was dry and eerie.

"Wh-Who is this?" Lisa looks at Tommy with wide eyes and a blank face. The voice comes again.

"When a fire burns, it sparks. And when it dies, there is only Ash. Heed my words Lisa Mays."

"I-I don't... I don't understand. What are you talking about, who is this, your scaring me?" Lisa has raised her voice considerably and now her mother has joined them in the living room. Tommy glances at her and then grabs the phone.

"Who is this, and why are you scaring my girlfriend?" Tommy grips the phone tightly and the veins in his neck poked out slightly as he yells into the receiver.

"You may see them by night, when the moon beams full over the valley, which shall smell of death! Death Tommy Critton, death!"

Tommy begins to reply and hears the line disconnect. He holds in a few curse words and replaces them with a frustrated grunt. As he hangs up the phone, Lisa's mom settles in next to her and hugs her neck. Critton sits opposite and comforts her as well. A few seconds pass and the young lady insists she is fine, just a little shaking up. Now Mrs. Mays inquires about what had been said, Lisa and Tommy explain what the mystery caller had told them. The three try to make something of the whole thing but came up with nothing. Eventually all returns to normal, mom goes back in the kitchen, and the young lovers finish watching Wheel of Fortune.

Derek Lastings scoops his little boy into his tired arms and hugs him tightly. Brad laughs then yells to get down and go play again. No one brings the subject of the book or Seth Wake back up, though Derek can tell by looking at his wife something is wrong. She gives him the look that says "don't ask" and he decides to leave it at that. Michael and his two friends head to the back door and outside. Josie takes her book upstairs to look through a bit more, maybe find out more about this witch, Alise Wake.

Michael pulls the back door closed behind him as the group walks out to the shed his dad had built. They each select a cinder block from the pile of bricks lying astray and take a seat. Matthew Turry puts his face in his hands along with his elbows on his knees ending up looking like a little boy who had been scolded and sent to his room. Steven Mass sits up straight, rubbing his head as if he has a bad headache. Michael on the other hand, rests his hands in his lap as he lets his eyes settle on a spider spinning its web on the empty doghouse setting a few steps away.

"So, what are you guys thinking about? I mean, about this whole situation." Mass continues to rub his head while he looks to the others for an answer. Matthew kind of shrugs his shoulders, then looks to Mike for his input.

"Well, I'm not quite sure yet. But, remember what that guy said at the basketball court?" Steve and Matt nod their heads. "Well, if we want answers, that's how we get them. The next full moon, we go to the valley and see what we can find?"

Steven stops rubbing his head and looks at Lastings uneasily. "We might not like what we find, and other than that, there must be two dozen valleys in Trench. How could we possibly find the one he spoke of?"

"Yeah, Steven does have a point. I mean, if that guy you seen at the ball court really does have fangs, well, I don't want to find him. And on top of all that, he could be the guy going around killing off the city. No thanks man."

Michael rolls his eyes at Matt and turns back to Steven. "I think I can find it. Somehow, I think I know exactly where to go, and how to get there. Now, I thought about what we might find myself, but if we kept well hidden, we could see what there is to see, and split. So, come on Steve, what do you say. The next full moon is tomorrow night, lets do it man!"

Steven shifts a bit and again looks quite uneasy. "If you are intent on going Michael, I'm with you. Not cause I want to be, just cause your a friend."

Matthew Turry shakes his head, "Well, I'm sorry guys, but you can count me out. I aint going anywhere near that guy again, or the they he seems to be talking about."

"That's fine Matt, between Steven and myself, we'll be all right. Its set then, tomorrow night!"

Down a short gravel drive through a midst of trees and brush, a double wide trailer sits in the middle of a level clearing. It's nothing fancy, not even for a trailer. The paneling is brown and an ugly yellow stripe runs along the side of it. Within it, all the way to the back in a room too small to be a bedroom, Barry Spencer sits on his bed staring blankly at the wall. He has always been known as the bad boy of Trench High, though you would not know it to see him now. Tears run down his dirty face and his hands tremble as he holds them between his knees. The home is empty besides him, his mother at one of her two jobs and the father God knows where getting drunk off the scale again. Barry thinks back merely hours before when he had been walking with his two best and only friends. Then everything seemed a blur until Seth Wake had gone, leaving him out of breath and his two friends dead. Spencer had kept his place for a good five minutes after Wake left. Finally he gained his breath back and pulled to his feet. Immediately he began to feel sick to his stomach as he looked at Larry lying there in a heap covered in blood. He was dead, and Barry knew it. As for Kevin Riley, there seemed to be a chance the blow wouldn't have killed him. At least from Spencer's point of view that is. He closed his eyes as he walked passed Stant and then jogged the rest of the way over to Kevin. The broken boy lied there next to an old oak tree on his belly and his face in the dirt. The bad boy of Trench High remembered how he had called to his friend, still trying to be the bad ass.

"Yo Kevin, c'mon man. Get up and let's go finish that freak." Barry nudged his friend with his foot and after not getting a response knelt down beside him. "Yo Kevin, are you, are you all right man?" He began to hear his own voice waver, his friend still lay still before him. Barry would never forget the sight of Kevin Riley when he turned him over. His eyes were wide open, as if he were staring at him. Blood had run from the boy's mouth and the looseness in the neck made it obvious it had been snapped. Spencer almost screamed, he opened his mouth to and when he did he got sick right there next to his dead friend. Next, Barry Spencer ran, he ran a full mile and a half back to his house. He ran through the front door, locked it behind him, then went to the bathroom and puked again.

Now, he is here, sitting on his bed trying to erase the reruns going on in his head. Wishing his mom would come home, crying, scared and alone.

Josie Lastings still flips though her book while her brother and friends converse out next to the garage. She has read the whole passage on Alise Wake and found something else very interesting. After the battle between Joseph Critton and the witch had ended, a necklace had been found around Alise's neck. The chain appeared to be as old as time itself as it was made of heavy silver. The charm hanging from this was a simple A, made from a rare substance known as ocean sandis. Yes, generally it looked like your typical sand, although, sandis could not be broken apart in your hand, or hammer for that matter. It happened to be the second hardest mineral on the planet at the time. Now days,

Sandis could not be found in any part of the world to the best of the books knowledge. Josie assumed the A stood for Alise, which actually makes a lot of since. And she likely never would know the actual meaning, Abraham.

The sun has slowly begun to fall on the horizon, and the girl knows darkness would soon be upon the land. She reads more about the Demons of the lake as well, until it began to spook her and she forces herself to close the book. The part that seems to bother her most comes out of the third paragraph of the story. It explains that, once the demons hear the child's voice, it surfaces and preys on the child. When done, the child's outside physical being remains, but the inside becomes the demon. She sits the book on the floor, then peers at the ceiling. From the smell of things, dinner would soon be done and Josie has an appetite tonight. She had not eating since lunch, so as you can imagine, the steaks cooking downstairs make her belly rumble. The young lady prepares to stand up and start for the stairs when the lights go out abruptly. She freezes in her tracks, scared to death. Fortunately, some light still shows through from outside and does give some comfort. Josie can hear her brother yelling about the lights down stairs. Brad does not even like it remotely dark in the house. Moments later, the lights flicker then come back on. After breathing a sigh of relief, she continues on her way down to the first floor. Michael meets her half way up the steps asking if she is all right. Josie giggles a little and tells him, "Of course silly, I wasn't even frightened." Michael knows better though, he can read his sister like a book. They walk together to the dining room table and then take a seat.

Derek picked up a large bowl of mashed potatoes along with a cup of gravy and carries it from the kitchen in to set the table. It did not happen often, though the man of the house helps out with dinner enough to keep Jennifer happy, and that is the important thing. She follows him in with the steaks and a pot of green beans. It would be the five of them for dinner, Steven and Matthew had other plans and had left a few minutes before the lights went out. After Derek makes another trip to the kitchen for the plates, everyone takes turns getting they're nightly glass of milk, then sits down to eat. As they do, Jennifer laughs a little as she picks up a plate. Ol dad had done it again, he forgot to get the silverware. Finally after ol mom retrieves the forks and knives, the group settles in for dinner.

Chapter 16

THE CAR RATTLES THIS way and that as Michael drives his Mustang down the dirt drive of Steven Mass. Dust fills the rear view mirror as the tires kick up dirt. The day had just recently turned to dusk. The full moon already could be found hanging high in the sky. Nearly a mile up the gravel drive is an old rancher that has recently been remodeled. It looks damn good for the year home it is. It has a front porch, but nothing to compare to that of the Lastings. The Mass house had more of a front step actually than a front porch. An outside light shines from over top the front door. When Michael parks the car and steps out, Rowdy comes running from out of his doghouse after him. The dog has a black coat and is a pure bread Shepard. The Lastings boy kneels down on one knee to greet him. Rowdy has become quite accustomed to Mike being around and not to mention, he loves the attention. Once done petting the dog, Michael walks up to the door and gives it a light knock. Within seconds, Steven shows up at the door ready and waiting to go. The two friends speak on the way back out to the car, scratch the dogs head one more time, and then they're off to the races.

"So how do we know where to look? Do you have any idea at all or are we just taking a stab at it?"

Mike twists his face a little as if to be thinking. "Well, I'll be honest with you Steve. For some strange off the wall reason, I feel like I know exactly where we are going. Go figure!"

Mass shrugs his shoulders, Michael turns his lights on and flips his blinker as he prepares to turn on to the main street, then burns the rear wheels as he hits pavement. Steven fidgets with the radio a bit until he finds one of his favorite tunes playing on the station. He sings along a little as he rolls down the passenger side window.

"If I go crazy then will you still call me super man? If I'm alive and well, will you be there holding my hand? Yeah, yeah, yeah!"

"Sing it Stevie!" Michael calls as he joins in on the fun. "I'll keep you by my side with my super human might, kryptonite, yeah, yeah, yeah." Lastings bangs his head a little more with each "yeah", Stevie taps the arm rest to the beat. The two friends have their own little concert in the comfort of Mike's car. Later, after a couple more songs come and go, the car slows and comes to a complete stop next to a thick patch of woods. Mass looks at his friend in bewilderment as he puts the car in park and gets out on the driver side.

"You coming, or are you gonna stay in the car?"

Steven does not reply as he steps from the car and begins to evaluate the situation. The area in which Michael wants to enter the woods looks like you would need a machete to work your way through it. After Michael retrieves a couple flashlights from the trunk, they attempt to enter. Both receive small scratches from a holly bush that had been unseen. The trees are thick and the light all but disappears once they make it a ways into the forest. Steven turns one of the two flashlights on and they struggle they're way further through an area of the woods that likely could be considered jungle. Mass follows Lastings until it begins to thin out a bit, then he steps to his side. The daylight seems to fade quicker by the second, soon all would be black except for the narrow passage illuminated by the flashlight. Michael still keeps his off in case the other decides to go they will have back up. Something moves in the distance, the leaves on the ground rustle furiously. Steven stops dead in his tracks, Michael follows suit. The noise continues on through the woods. At first the thing seems to be coming closer, then they could tell the steps led away as the rustling leaves fade into the darkening night.

At this point, both lights become turned on to try and light up more area. Thoughts of turning back fill the heads of both young men, but neither dared suggest it to the other. An hour of non-stop hiking bring them to a small clearing. To one side lay what is left of a campfire, on the other are pieces of chopped wood. Apparently this had recently been the perfect spot for a night out in the woods. Michael could even see where the stakes had been driven into the ground to hold the tent. Of course the spot had been cleared, though the evidence remained.

"Where..., Steven began to say then trailed off to catch his breath. "Where on God's green earth are we Michael. And how do you have any idea we are going the right way."

Lastings does not answer, he simply stands there in his green sweatshirt and blue jean pants surveying the area. He has a wild look in his eye that seems to tell a story, not that Steven could read it. A minute passes before any more words are said and when Mike does speak, he sounds blank and lost in another world.

"I know where to go. Right this way, it's as if I am being told. As if I am being led. Right this way!"

Steven looks on as the oldest of the Lastings off spring peers into the dark surrounding before him. And moments later, he takes off back into the woods and away from the clearing. This time, Mass has right much difficulty keeping up. It seems as if Michael had been given a mission and with no time to spare. Another forty-five minutes or so and the two friends find themselves peering out over a bearing valley. A stench seems to rise up from the ground and a mist filled with mysteria covers the ground. Steven becomes quite scared, Michael on the other hand acts calm and collective, like he knew he had to be there.

"This is the spot, this is the valley the guy spoke of when we were playing basket ball. I mean, I can feel the evil, and I can feel the power in the air. Something brought us here Steve, I know it." Lastings turned off his flashlight, laid it at his feet, then stuffed his hands in his pocket.

"Um, your acting a little strange man, are you sure your all right?" Again Steven does not get an answer. So he switches his light to the off position as well and gets down on one knee to wait out the silence. It had been darn near two and a half hours since these two had left the Mustang. Now, again they waited two more. Steven eventually sits down and leans his head against a nearby tree. Michael never flinches, he only stands there solemnly with his hands in his pockets, watching and waiting. Now darkness has completely filled the sky, the only light comes off the full moon shining above. The smell in the air quickly becomes worse, turning to that of what Steven had feared most, the smell of death. At about the time three shadows forms from afar, Michael snaps out of his little trance.

"Holy shit," he whispers, "Let's get back a little and see what happens. They don't know were here and I want it to stay that way." Steven gets up to his feet and follows his friend back into the woods a little bit.

"Good to have you back, I was lonely for a good while there. So tell me Dorothy, how is Oz?"

Michael snickers a bit then both keep quiet as they watch the three figures stalk there way down the center of the valley. As the moonlight hits Ambrose's face, the two friends immediately recognize him and take a step back. Soon the three near the end of the valley and come to a stop. Slowly they double over and go to all fours. Seconds later, three wolves emerge, running separate ways into the forest. The black wolf scampers directly for Michael and Steven. They panick, turning to run Mass trips and takes a hard fall. Michael disappears into the darkness, dropping his flashlight on the way. Steve fights off the pain and gets to his feet like a shot from a gun. He does not look back, only breaks into a sprint as if he were to take first in the fifty-yard dash. The light fumbles in his hands, though he eventually gets it to come on. The light helps him see his way though another impossible maze of trees. Him and Michael will never be able to catch back up with each other now. The important thing would be for both of them to make tracks as quick as possible. Mass makes it a pretty good distance before an owl takes flight from a tree ahead. The sound of flapping wings and the hoot from the animal's mouth about causes his heart to skip a beat. Though, he continues on, and maybe luck has been on his side this night, but he finds his way out to the road. About a quarter mile up from where his friends Mustang sits awaiting they're return.

Michael Lastings scrambles his way along, bumping into trees and outstretched branches. One branch catches the boy across the face leaving a nice gouge across his forehead. That mixed in with the sweat pouring off his head sends a stinging sensation through him that rocks his whole body. Moments later, Lastings catches his knee on a stump, it takes a nice chunk from his leg and now he finds himself in the same position Steven Mass had been in only minutes before, face first on the ground. The pain could not be shot out, a look of agony shows deeply in young Michael's face. He tries to get up and finds it to be to no avail. So he lays as he is for minutes on end. The night has turned deadly silent, and the dark has engulfed everything into a nightmarish blackness. Michael Lastings lets the pain go its course a little while longer, then pulls himself to his feet. All at once the sounds of the forest resume. Suddenly, he can feel eyes upon him, and leaves begin to rustle. Very slowly, Mike begins to move forward again, away from the sound of the leaves. But now the thing is upon him, he can feel its hot breath against his legs. A spot of moonlight finds its way through the trees as Lastings continues to back away ever so slightly. The creature before him turns out to be the black wolf in which they had encountered in the valley earlier. It snarls and lunges itself into the young man ahead. Both roll to the ground, the wolf goes for Mike's neck with its teeth. Luckily the kid gets his arm up in time, the jaws of the beast's mouth clamp onto his forearm. Lastings screams with agony, and tries to find something, anything to get this thing off him. His loose hand falls upon a fallen tree branch. Michael swings it with all he has left, the black wolf yelps and falls when the thick limb catches it across its neck and head. Soon the animal returns to its feet and seemingly runs off. Lastings once again struggles to his feet, blood spewing from his arm. His knee has been busted up pretty bad as well, and the scratches on his face sting worse than ever.

"Steven, Steven are you out there?"

There would be no reply. Michael again sluggishly moves onward. Every few minutes he calls for Steven, hoping to get an answer. Nothing comes from the blackness, at least, nothing from Steven Mass that is. From out of the darkness steps Seth Wake, his eyes glowing in the night. Michael recognizes him, but not at first. It takes him a moment or two to realize where he had seen this guy.

"Why, your car of course. I dropped the cigarette in your floorboard. It pains me to the bone you don't remember Michael Lastings. Right to the bone." Seth has a smirk, the kind we all would like to slap right off the smart ass at work. Michael looks deep into Wakes eyes, something inside them plays like a movie on a TV. screen.

"You led me here, you led me to the valley. Thats how I knew exactly where to go."

Wake does not answer his question, only continues on with his own business. "I need your help Michael. There is something I must do and cannot do it alone. So I have chosen you as the one."

"I wouldn't help you if you were drowning and I had the life preserver. So forget it. You can choose someone else, or for that matter, go straight to hell!" Michael clenches his good hand into a fist and takes a hard swing at Seth's face. Seth catches the blow with cat like reflexes and turns Mikes arm behind his back. Another sharp pain shoots through his body. Another scream fills the forest. Lastings collapses, Seth stands over him, his shadow down casting on the spot that Michael lay. The fallen man scrambles to sit up, Wake grabs him by the throat and with one hand and yanks Lastings back to his feet. The poor kid's body has become a wreck, the only thing keeping him from falling again is the icy grip of Seth Wake's hand around his throat. And then the teeth, those fangs are revealed again. Michael closes his eyes!

Chapter 17

Josie Lastings rolls over one final time and decides it is past time to get out of bed. The alarm clock reads quarter to ten o'clock. She sits up slowly and rubs her eyes. A slight chill runs up her bare legs as her nightgown stops just short of her knees. Josie keeps telling herself she's going to start sleeping in her pajamas, but she hasn't listened yet. It's tough to get out of the warm bed and up into the cool air in her room. Upon doing so, Lastings strolls over to an oak dresser then pulls out the bottom drawer. The young lady sorts through a few things before removing a pair of blue jeans and slipping them on. Downstairs the air is warmer, the Saturday morning cartoons can be heard from with in the living room. Little Brad appears to be glued to the screen as Elmer Fudd chases Bugs Bunny down the rabbit hole. Josie only pauses for another moment then trudges sleepily into the kitchen for a bite to eat. The kitchen floor feels like ice with out any socks on. The girl ignores it and swings open the cupboard door. Frosted Flakes, Special K, Marshmallow Maties, and Golden Grahams all seem to stare back at her as she eyes the choices before her. She thinks to herself, *All right, we have dad's cereal, mom's, little brothers, and Michael's favorite. So much for that idea!* Josie rolls her eyes as she shuts the cupboard and takes a peripheral view of the counter. The toaster sits directly next to the stove, then comes the bread of course. Also, stacked up toward the back of the counter lays a box of nutri-grain bars, Rice Krispee treats, Carnation Instant Breakfast, cinnamon rolls, doughnut sticks, and let's not forget the Eggo waffles someone had forgot to put back in the freezer.

After throwing the blueberry flavored waffles back in the freezer, grabbing a couple of nutri-grain bars, and pouring a tall glass of Instant Breakfast, Josie turns to the dining room and has a seat at the dining room table. Looking out the window and into the side yard, she can see that her dad is at it already. Derek had told her he planned on having a barbecue. His daughter is mostly surprised to find him setting up the grill already. *It's not even noon yet!*

In the living room, Bugs has taking a leave and now Daffy Duck appears on the screen throwing one of his famous tantrums. Brad has not moved an inch.

"Hey Bradford, where's mom at? Still in the bed?"

No answer would come, at least not now, it seems as if he never even heard her.

"Brad!" Josie calls again, "Hey you, turn around here for a minute." Finally the boy does hear his sister, he turns around to listen to what she has to say.

"Where's mom at, I've called you twice now."

Brad crumples his face, "I dunno, me thinks mama outside." And right away the boy hurls his attention back to the television. Josie takes another bite of her strawberry nutri-grain bar, followed by a couple swallows of her chocolate shake. (At least that's what Carnation calls it) It turns out to be a lazy morning. Josie ends up sitting or laying the hours away. It turns out her mother had hit the grocery store for the bare essentials of a barbecue. You know, hot-dogs and hamburgers, buns to go along with them, potato chips, etc.

About two in the afternoon, people begin to show up for the barbecue. Derek's boss arrives first followed by a few other of his fellow employees he has invited. Tommy Critton and Lisa Mays come a few minutes before three. Josie is out in the side yard putting a tablecloth over the old rugged picnic table. Her father has told her the food will be ready in a few minutes and that they could start bringing out the side dishes. It feels a bit odd grilling out halfway through the month of October, but no one seems to mind all that much.

Jennifer Lastings closes the CD player and pushes the play button softly. Moments later, Alabama comes on singing "Five o'clock five hundred." This has always been her favorite group and everyone else seemed to enjoy them as well. Derek and his boss stood across the yard talking about the latest deliveries at the warehouse. Josie tears open a bag of Dorritos and begins to snack. Tommy and Lisa sip on their sodas and Derek's other friends from work stand in a small group telling dirty jokes. The party seems to be in full swing by this time, the music flowing, a gentle breeze carries the smell of cooked meat across the yard, and the sun has even poked its head out from behind the clouds. Alabama sings away on the portable boom box, the first song ends and next comes "Keeping Up" followed by "How do you fall in Love?" The fourth track on the CD happens to be "Tennessee River", everyone joins in once Josie starts singing along. Soon thereafter, the group gets rowdy and even Derek finds himself hooting and hollering with the rest of the guys. About this time, Michael pulls up in the front yard with Steven Mass in the driver seat. The two friends can tell right away that the party is jumping. Steven hops out of the passenger side followed by Michael on the driver's side. Stephen jogs up the stairs and into the side yard. Michael walks slowly behind him, trying not to make it obvious he had taken a chunk out of his leg the night before. As always, Jennifer rushes over to greet her oldest son and informs him that plenty of food still has to be eating. That turns out to be good news for both young men as neither of them had eating all day. When Mother gets done with Michael, his sister along with Lisa and Tommy comes over. Josie still dances a little in place, left over from the rush she had only moments before.

"So, I heard what you guy's planned to do last night, so spill it fellows. Did you go, what happened? Did you see anything or anyone?" Josie speaks so quickly you almost can not understand what she has said. Michael catches it though and answers immediately.

"Well, settle in because this is a whopper." Mike leads the gang over to the back fence, away from most of the crowd, then leans up against one of the supports. "I picked Steven up and we drove out not really knowing where we were going to end up. Eventually I parked the car on the side of the road next to a patch of thick brush and we exited the vehicle, retrieved a couple flashlights and followed our noses through the forest. We came...

Steven breaks in, "You mean followed your nose, this guy was like stoked. Mystified or something!"

"Anyway, Michael begins again, we came to this clearing where apparently someone had camped the night before. And yes, something did come over me, like I had been lead there or something. So finally we come to the valley in which this guy apparently spoke about at the basket ball court."

"A valley?" Tommy interrupts. "You mean like what the guy said when he called Lisa and scared her half to death?"

Michael turns his head and he, his sister and Steve in unison ask, "What phone call?" The three look on with wide eyes waiting and wondering what other pieces of the puzzle this will add. Critton looks at Lisa puzzled.

"You didn't tell them about the phone call, I thought sure you guys would know by now!"

Lisa looks down at her feet and mumbles something the rest could not make out. Then when asked to repeat herself the girl lifts her chin and speaks slow and clear.

"I just thought you would think of it as silly and kind of laugh it off. I mean, I don't have much of an idea whats going on, and maybe none of you do either. But you know more than I do and I guess that's why I didn't say anything."

Steven Mass looks to Mike to give a reply, he says nothing. Now Steve looks to the rest of the teenagers around him and decides he will be the one to speak up.

"Well the truth is, we don't know all that much. We didn't know last night before we went out to the valley, and we don't know any more after venturing there last night. Make note of this though, whoever they are, or whatever they are, they mean business." Steve pauses a moment, takes in a deep breath and goes on. "Anyway, I 'm curious about the phone call even if no one else is. Would you mind telling us about it?"

Lisa doesn't see any harm in this so she lets them have it, right there out on the table. Here it is, apples? oranges? it really doesn't matter either way! After about ten minutes or so, they finish up on the phone call and turn back to Michael to reiterate his own story.

"All right, so we get to the valley and this stench is coming up in the air. It was a horrible smell, I don't think I could explain it even if you all wanted me to try. So the next thing we know, three dark figures appear in the moonlight at the far end of the valley. Now here comes the spooky and amazing part. They began to walk the valley and at one point we recognized one of the three guys, it was the one from the ball court. Next, they suddenly go down on all fours, and you don't have to believe me cause I know what I seen, they went from men to wolves. And in the blink of an eye, the black one tore after us. Steven fell when we turned to run, but luckily he made it out. I on the other hand had a good head start. I'm not exactly sure what happened to Steven at this point but I can tell you this. I had a hell of a time getting out of there. I swear I could feel the wolf's breath on the back of my neck, weird considering it was on all fours and I was on my feet. Somehow or another though, I lost the wolf, or I should say he turned away. From there on out, I followed what seemed to be a partial path, with the help of my flashlight of course, and it led me on out to the road."

"Damn guys, you shouldn't be the only ones having fun around here, how about next time you plan on going vampire hunting you invite good ol Tommy along with you?" Everyone laughs at Tommy with the exception of Michael, his mind is elsewhere. If Steve had looked close enough at just that moment, he might have seen the blankness in his friend's eyes. Hell if anyone had been paying more attention they might have noticed it. Yet, then it was gone, and the eldest of the Lastings children snapped back to reality when his mother came walking up.

"Hey you guys! Throwing your own party huh, well is it open to anyone or only those with invitation are welcome." Jennifer laughs, they all laugh, even Michael this time. "Would one of you like to run to the store, it seems were running low on ice... and soda for that matter."

"Sure mom," Josie calls. Michael decides he will be the one to drive and as for Lisa, Tommy, and Steven, they decide to "hang out" until their friends return.

Michael quickly walks around front and hops in his old Mustang, Josie follows somewhat sluggishly behind him. They roll the windows about half way down and Michael pushes the power button on his CD player. Josie looks on as her brother selects a particular song then turns up the volume. After a few seconds, Aerosmith's "Walk this Way" fills the interior of the car. Josie smiles, brother and sister are out cruising again. Even if it is as simple as a trip to the grocery store, its cruising. She thinks back to the many times her and Michael along with some of his or her friends got together and just went for a ride. Of course Mike did all the driving, so Josie got to handle most of the music. The summer nights were warm and everyone drove with their windows down. Now, that didn't make a difference here in Trench, but once they got out to Spontania there would be plenty of people to hoop and holler at. Now, on the way to the grocery store, Josie found it almost funny, but her brother never forgot how she loved to play that song as the last song of the night. Kind of the kicker of the evening if you will.

The car makes its way through the lot of the store and comes to rest in a parking spot right up front of the building. Josie races out of the passenger side seat, up to the walk, passes the pay phone and soda machines, passes the commercialized bench and almost into the store before stopping to wait on Michael. Now it would be her turn to wait on him, what goes around comes around. Michael works his way up to almost the bench with the commercial ads on it and stops dead in his tracks. Josie looks at him a little awkward before realizing he is staring at the ground as if it had just jumped up and bit him.

"Did you see that,? It was only for a second, but I know I seen a black cat, it ran right out from under this bench."

"Eh, well, no I didn't see anything. It probably just a late night snack coming back to haunt you or something. C'mon, lets get the stuff we need and get back to the party."

So they do, Michael grabs the sodas and Josie fetches the ice. On the way back home they listen to the radio. And when VanHalen's "Running with the Devil" comes on, the blood starts pumping. Josie dances and sings along while Michael steadily presses on the accelerator. Good songs have a tendency to do that to the best of us. When they arrive home, it is Elvis playing on the boom box and the alcohol has been passed out. Michael decides to have himself a brewski, as for Josie, she settles for a whine cooler. As she sips on her drink, Josie watches on as dad and his work buddies try to play a game of badminton. *You don't have to be 21 to have fun, hell, I'm having a ball here at 17.* She chuckles to herself then decides to get up for another helping of hot-dogs and potato chips.

Michael Lastings sits to the side of the yard up close to the house, but away from the area where people come in and out. Steven has somehow made his way into the badminton game and this leaves Mike almost secluded. A blank expression comes over his face and within a seconds time, it was the night before. Seth Wake stared him in the eyes, his body felt battered and bruised. Wake had said he needed Michael's help, he needed him for something. Mike had turned him down, had told him to find someone else, and then, and then... what? Michael wasn't sure what had happened, he vaguely remembers Seth bearing his teeth, but then all is black, and all is gone!

Chapter 18

THE PARTY HAD GONE very well, so good in fact that Michael has yet to recover. A little too much grease for one night. He could feel a strong burning sensation in the lower part of his chest and was having horrible gas. He thought if it did not stop soon he would have to break out one of his Glade air-freshener. Lastings sits up from his recliner then pulls himself to his feet. A half a glass of cherry Kool-Aid sits on the table next to his chair. The television remote has been placed next to it. Michael glances down at it and then over to the television. The little white bear on the screen raves over Snuggle fabric softener. Mike decides he will leave the TV on, so there would at least be some sound in the house, then slowly lumbers into his tiny kitchen.

Lastings finds himself looking around the room for a moment realizing how badly it needs to be cleaned. Piles of junk mail sit on the table along with an unfinished bowl of cereal from that morning. The dishes in the sink over flow to the counter and a litter of sugar lightly surfaces the counter. He stands like this for quite some time, he feels like the walk from the living room to the kitchen had taking any amount of energy he still had. The truth of it all though is simple, he is not looking forward to getting started on his evening choirs. And the heartburn is not helping matters any, of course neither does the sensation that he will fill his drawers every time he passes gas.

It finally takes the ringing of the phone took get the young man moving again. After three rings, Michael picks up. "Hello?"

Silence literally floods the ear piece, and it leaves him uneasy. Quiet should never be so loud. Then the voice comes. "Good evening Michael, this is your good friend Seth Wake. You haven't forgotten me again so soon have you?"

"No, I'm afraid I couldn't forget such an ugly face as your own Wake, I aint that lucky." Michael speaks fiercely into the phone, raising his voice with as he goes. "What the hell do you want, why don't you just leave me the fuck alone?"

Seth pauses on the other end, knowing it bothers the man he's speaking with to no end having to wait for a reply. "Temper, temper Mikey. I just thought I would call and see if you wanted help with the dishes, you know, you wash and I'll dry!"

Michael's blood begins to boil, the games this guy is playing are wearing thin on his nerves. His mind becomes filled with anger, and the oldest of the Lastings children cant help but think back to the last time he had been so pissed off. It had been soon after his seventeenth birthday. His mom and dad had given him the Mustang he owns to this day only two weeks prior to what happened. At the time the paint job had been mint and the boy had begin driving it back and forth to school. It happened on a Tuesday afternoon, the day before Mike had gotten in Jerome Barrel's face for pushing him as they passed in the hall. Jerome had acted like a big shot then. But when they were supposed to meet after school the following day, Michael came out to find his car keyed Pepsi -Cola poured all over his beautiful paint job. It was never proven that Jerome Barrel had done this unscrupulous act. Michael Lastings knew though, yes, he knew the son of a bitch had done it. So he sought revenge, and one day while in Phi's Ed in a game of basketball, Mike let Barrel have it. He waited until the jackass went up for one of his "famous jump shots", and gave him a good hard shove. Jerome Barrel came down with a thud as he landed and his head snapped back and hit the hard wood floor hard. It almost busted him open. Michael, naturally got suspended for his behavior. Of course, that didn't matter then, and hell, it didn't matter now. The little fuck had deserved it!

His attention turns back to the phone receiver, this guy would deserve what Michael intends to do to him as well. "Listen, you may have gotten a lucky shot in the other night, last night I mean... that don't mean it will happen next time. You damn near broke my arm, and for what. What do you want? What do I have that you could possibly want dam it?" Tears begin to well up in the corner of the young man's eyes. His heart pounds, sweat has begun to pour from out of his pores and the heartburn has been forgotten for now. Only anger remains. Anger lined with the slightest bit of fear, which seems quickly to be turning into a lot of fear.

Seth Wake again pauses, this time he waits a little longer before he speaks. "Life, Michael, I want your life blood." Another pause. "Look out your kitchen window Michael Lastings. I'm watching you!"

The icy finger that had went up Lastings back earlier, now returns. He shivers and looks down at his trembling hands, the phone quivers in his right and his left shakes as he lifts it to the air and examines it. Michael realizes his breath has caught up in his lungs and exhales with what might appear as an exaggerated burst. Slowly he turns his head to the window, focusing in on what might be lurking inches beyond the glass. Nothing. Seth has to be playing with his mind, he couldn't really be there. Michael takes baby steps to the kitchen sink and peers out into the darkness of his back yard. A face appears as suddenly as the strike of a snake. Seth Wake's face. Mike jumps back and almost finds himself on the floor, but regains his balance.

Then the anger returns again, Michael's face turns bright red. He snatches the plastic bowl off his old wooden kitchen table then heaves it at the window. It strikes the glass and the spoon along with the remaining milk and cereal (Golden Grahams) shoot out in every direction. The bowl itself falls first to the counter then comes to rest with the rest of dishes at the sink. Any other day this may have been comical to him, not now. He charges over to the drawer with his kitchen utensils in it and withdraws a steak knife from within. Seconds later, Michael saunters out the front door, and stalks towards the rear of the house. The darkness seems to thicken as he goes, so thick he feels he will choke on it. A shadow moves in the distant starlight, now the boy breaks into a sprint.

Michael finds nothing in the back yard when he finally stops chasing the shadow. He bends forward and places his hands on his knee's, his breaths come short and sharp. Something snaps a few yards to his right. Mike thinks it came from over next to the water well. Quickly he quiets his breathing, listening for the smallest of sounds. He can hear the sound of water trickling from the well wall, it has done that since he moved into the house. And there is something else, breathing. Again the Lastings boy goes for the thing in the darkness.

He has it!

He has hold of something, and then nothing. A quick twist and something sharp to his shoulder and Michael falls to the ground, his back only inches from the well wall. Something slimy splatters up on his face and clothes. Mud, the ground never dried out this far due to the constant seepage of the well. He scurries back to his feet, the knife he had taking from the kitchen gone. His clothes feel cold and wet, and heavy.

Michael trudges back inside, he closes and locks the door behind him and goes into his bedroom. The shirt peels off his back like a layer of old skin. Next he looks down, finding his shoes caked in mud. Beyond where he stood were muddy footprints that lead from his bedroom back out to the front room.

"FUCK," fuck me! God Dam it, I'm gonna kill you Seth Wake." Michael screams into his empty house, the sound of his voice floats out to the yard too, it also is empty, and has been the whole time. "I'm gonna fucking kill you Wake. I'm gonna kill you! DO YOU HEAR ME YOU SON OF A BITCH!"

Michael properly disposes of his soiled clothes and sits his sneakers in the kitchen to be cleaned up later. He likes his showers hot, so as the water streams down from the shower head and falls over his body, steam lifts to the ceiling. The water feels good to the skin, good and warm. The heartburn has returned but doesntt seem all too bad at the moment. As for the gas, it seems to have subsided. Michael lets himself slide down the blue tiled wall and come to rest sitting on the tub floor. The water still falls on his head, neck, and shoulder's, and for the moment, he feels relaxed and calm. The feeling doesnt last long, only until he gets out of the shower. After washing up, he removes the towel from the bar on the back of the bathroom door. A big, blue worn out rag is what it appears to be, but it seems to do the job. Next, Lastings steps from the tub and stands in front of the steam-covered mirror. He rests one hand on the corner of the sink and prepares to wipe the fogged up mirror.

When he does, its not his reflection staring back at him. Not at all, it is the face of the lady in Josie's book. Michael screams and like before jumps back. This time he doesnt keep his balance. He goes backwards, his legs catch the rim of the bathtub and he spills into it, hitting his head on the wall as he goes down. The pain seems to shoot from his head to his feet and back again. Michael grabs the back of his head and lays over on his side, now in the fetal position. His heart pounds in his head, the room seems to be spinning around and around. He closes his eyes tighter, it doesnt help. Dizziness begins to over take him and suddenly he feels sick to his stomach. And...

Michael looked up at his dad, his hero munching on cotton candy. Mom stood opposite of him holding his little sister's hand. Just the four of them and not a care in the world. They all loved the stated fair and went every year it arrived, if at all possible. Derek Lastings held his boys hand, maybe eight years old had been a little to old for holding hands, Michael liked it though. His dad lowered his other arm so that Michael could get some of that good ole' cotton candy. Then, the little boy walking beside his dad looked over to the right hand side of the midway.

"Oh wow," he exclaimed. "Daddy, I want to ride that space ship. It looks totally rad!"

"I don't know Michael, that may be a little much for you, what do you think honey?" Derek said as he looked to his wife for support. She took a good look at the ride before them and started to say no when...

"Mom, please say yes, please. You and Josie can go on those swings over there. And dad and me can go on the space ship. Please mom, please."

Jennifer Lastings looked at her son's pleading face and then faced his sister. "Would you like to go on the swings?" The words no more and came out of her mouth and Josie shook her head yes. "all right then, have fun you guy's. And so Michael and his dad got on the space ship.

It started out slow, then faster and faster and faster still it spun like a top. Little Michael quickly discovered he didn't like this ride, hated it in fact. When it finally ended, Derek helped his son walk out since he seemed too dizzy to manage himself. Moments later, Michael's eye's began to stop and his stomach churned. And then he began to throw up. Cotton candy, hot dogs, the soda's, all of it came back up as the poor boy puked again and again.

"Ow, ow shit." Michael says groggily as he tries to lift his head. The stench of regurgitated food fills his senses and the young man realizes he is lying in it, his own puke. Very, very slowly, he sits up and gets himself together. He would have one hell of a bump on his head come morning. What time is it for that matter. Oh well, he has more cleaning up to do, and this time he'd do it without a peek in the mirror. When he gets in bed that night, he sleeps like a rock. Not even his sister calling at two am. causes him to budge.

By seven-thirty, almost everyone has gone on home and the party has been cleaned up for the most part. Josie thinks it would be a good idea to go to the mall in Spontania. Lisa agrees to go with her and the two girls decide they like Tommy's idea of them going by themselves, just the two of them. Lisa seems a little reluctant at first, then agrees. Tommy drives the girls out with the understanding that he would have to pick them up at nine, when the mall closes. The ride out seems long and drawn out, even though they exceed the speed limit most of the way. The parking lot looks to be quite full. Tommy thinks. Maybe him not tagging along turned out for the best. After all, he wouldn't have to fight for a parking spot or anything. All he had to do was drop the girls at the door and make tracks.

Lisa kisses Tommy, then she turns briskly and walks, almost strutting, into the mall with Josie. They have only looked in a few stores when they spot Craig Johnson leaning against the wall of American Eagle. Josie stops in her tracks and looked at Lisa.

"I don't believe it, he's by himself. Should I go talk to him, I mean this may be my only chance."

Lisa giggles and shakes her head, "Go for it if you like girl, but I've warned you about him before. All he wants is a piece of the pie, and it doesn't matter what flavor it is as long as it looks good and tasty."

Josie laughs, "Yes Ms. Mays. Of course Ms. Mays, and don't forget, necking leads to sex."

Both girls have a good laugh, then Josie separates from her best friend and starts toward her biggest crush. She takes her jacket off and swings it over her shoulder. Then she starts into her sexiest, strutting your stuff walk, she has to offer. After lifting her chest up and out she unzips the front of her sweater so that you can see the start of her cleavage. Craig, who has been looking the other way at some blond in fish net stockings turns around to find Josie Lastings heading his way. The expression on his face when he sees her and looks her up and down is enough to make Josie melt, she doesn't let it show though. The jock runs his fingers through his hair and then stares the girl up and down again. This time his eyes fall on her chest where they hesitate before reaching Josie's eyes. His eyes boar into hers, she feels butterflies in her stomach and all at once she feels like something is pushing out from her insides at every point of her body.

"What's up girl? Josie Lastings if my memory doesn't fail me. It never does when it comes to a hot body though."

Josie does her best to hide the blushing, and does a great job at keeping up the front she's putting on. "Your memory is holding up perfectly. And as far as this hot body, well, you have no idea babe." Her voice flows without a quiver, but the girl can feel the foundations shaking and isn't sure how long she can keep it up.

"Oh don't you worry Ms. Lastings, I've seen enough of your skimpy little numbers you like to wear to know it's sweet as sugar. So, what do you say we grab a little popcorn and a snack and catch the late show. That is, if your not afraid of the dark."

Josie opens her mouth to reply and nothing comes out. She swallows the lump in her throat and tries to get it back together.

Come on Josie, don't screw up now. It's just starting to get good! Just breathe in, and back out.

This time, everything comes out fine. "Ha, the darker it is, the better. I have to warn you though, I bite!"

"Mmm, well, the movie's on me. But let me warn you, I bite back." With that, Craig waves his hand out in front as if to say, ladies first. Josie turns slowly, giving her most sensuous look out of the corner of her eyes as she does. As she begins to walk, Craig quickly catches up and joins her side. He puts his hand on the small of her back and Josie feels the butterflies get worse.

Lisa gets the picture and smiles, she's happy for her friend, she only hopes the girl knows what she's getting herself into.

After a good long wait, the theater lights begin to dim and Josie feels herself begin to shake a little. She bites her lip and takes a deep breath. Now all is dark with the exception of the glowing screen, and Josie realizes she is scared to death. She can't believe she is sitting next to Craig Johnson, and in a dark theater of all places. And then, a thought crosses her mind that frightens her even more.

What if he plans on taking me home? What if I have given him the wrong impression?

Lisa did her share of flirting herself while she looked in the different shops, nothing extreme though. She loved Tommy and wouldn't hurt him for the world. And even though she was alone, the time went by pretty quick. The last fifteen minutes seemed to drag on forever, but it wasn't that bad. When she sees Tommy pull up, she quickly pushes open the mall doors and runs out to the car. They wait for Josie until eleven-thirty, then decide she has caught a ride with Craig Johnson. And maybe in more than one way. So, both agree to head on home, and that Josie had most likely already left the mall anyway.

Josie almost loses her breath as Craig's tongue wrestles with her own. His hands have worked they're way up under her shirt and they feel wonderful against her breasts. One hand slides away and falls to her stomach and then her thigh. Josie rubs her hand up her crush's back and suddenly a thousand tingling sensations shoot all over her body as Johnson slides his hand from the girl's thigh up between her legs. Josie moans and hopes no one hears her, not that she really cares. Her hands drop to the back of Johnson's pants. Moments later, the girl moves her right hand to Craig's thigh and then further up the crotch of his pants. She has become quite hot between the legs at this point. Craig moves his hands to the zipper of Josie's jeans and the credits hit the screen. The lights begin to brighten and the two pull away from one another. She almost wishes the movie hadn't ended yet. Another few minutes and she's pretty sure her pants would have been wide open. Now, it is over. They stay for a minute, then Craig leads her out, his hand resting on her butt this time. When he goes the opposite direction from which Josie is supposed to meet Tommy and Lisa, she follows. A clock over one of the fountain's reads twenty after eleven. Josie ignores it and walks on.

The rest of the mall has all but closed. Soon Craig and Josie reach the opposite side of the mall. Johnson tells her to wait in the lobby while he goes for the truck. Once the door shuts behind him, Josie takes in a few deep breaths. Every part of her body seems to scream for Craig Johnson. She wants him pretty bad, but not tonight. No, not the first date. It wouldn't be right.

He wants to though, expects it for that matter. After all that shit you talked before the movie, and then tongue wrestling with him in the theater, you know he expects it!

A figure appears in the distance, and in the darkness, Josie thinks it to be Craig. The closer he gets though, the girl comes to realize the truth. This guy looks darker, almost eerie. When Ash steps onto the sidewalk, Josie lets out a muffled scream. He has fangs, sharp werewolf like fangs. Scared almost to death, the girl flees back into the mall. Everything seems to have been locked down, someone yells to her they are closing but Josie never slows down. She makes her way into a door marked "Employee's Only" and realizes she has found her way into a McDonald's kitchen. At the farthest counter in the back of the kitchen, the girl ducks down and gets to her knees and elbow's. All seems quiet for a while, and for a moment Beauty begins to feel safe from the Beast.

The door opens, the same one she had used to enter the McDonald's kitchen. Josie's heart sinks, her emotions are in an uproar. There she is horny as hell one second, and the whit's scared out of her the next. Lastings keeps her head down and tries her damnedest not to make a sound. She can her the boots click across the floor as they come closer. She wants to scream so bad it hurts, her body shakes from head to toe. Has she ever been so scared in her life?

The footsteps stop.

About half way into the kitchen.

Josie bites her hand to keep from screaming. Tears pour out of her eyes. She closes them, and tightly. And then the footsteps return. The click of the boot with every step. *Clik, clik, clik.*

On my God, I'm gonna die, I'm gonna die, God help me!

Then, like a slap to the face, Josie realizes the steps are falling away, not getting closer. And that, that is the door. Hes gone, it is gone. Now she can hold it back no longer, she sobs, crying out into the inner part of her elbow. She cries so hard, she almost cant catch her breath. Finally, she lets her self sprawl out in the floor, still crying, and almost exhausted.

Again, all is quiet. Not even the sound of a ticking clock. Josie lifts her head to look around. She fell asleep, cried herself to sleep actually. But how long has she been out. She couldn't be sure. As the girl moves her arm, pins and needles shoot though it. Lastings gets to her feet very quietly, and cautiously goes for the door. At first, she thinks she will never get the nerve up to open it, then with out even thinking, swings it open.

Still, all is quiet, and still.

Josie can't stand it, she has to get out, she leaves the doorway and begins to run. She runs as fast as her legs can carry her until she reaches the pay phones at the end of the food court. Her hands are shaking so bad she barely gets the change out of her pocket. After dropping a quarter in the slot, Josie dials her brother's number. Michael lives closer than anyone and would be able to get there the quickest. No one picks up, the phone rings four, five, six, seven times. No answer. Then, a shadow falls over her! Josie realizes she's trapped and begins to shriek. The sound echoes throughout the mall, but there is no one to hear, and no one to help.

Chapter 19

Jennifer Lastings is in her bedroom, she hugs a piece of her daughter's clothing to her chest. She is hunched over on her king size bed, sobbing, wishing it could be her daughter she was holding and not some damn shirt. Dark rings encircle her eyes, she has not slept all night. How could she with her daughter missing? Daybreak had hit about two hours before and Derek has been looking for Josie ever since. The mall had been his first destination. If he found her he would call, but the phone had not rung. They called Lisa's house in the middle of the night to see why Tommy had not brought their daughter home yet, they didn't like the reply. Apparently, Josie had hooked up with some guy she had a crush on and had given the impression she would get a ride home with him.

Jennifer hugged the fancy blue shirt tighter and again imagined her daughter in place of it. A sound from the other room breaks her concentration. The mother of three jumps as she hears a scraping noise flow in from the dining room. The sound comes again, this time a little louder, though it does not seem any closer. Jennifer cautiously stands up from her bed and crosses the room. She pauses at the doorway and listens for the noise again.

All is quiet.

Jennifer tiptoes her way out of her bedroom and through the hallway to the dining room. As she is about to turn the corner, the noise comes again. She feels her stomach shrink as she jumps back behind the wall.

Screech *Screech!*

Jennifer swallows the lump in her throat and slowly peeks around the corner. As she does her eyes widen as she finds...

Her son.

Bradford is standing directly in front of the fish tank with a fork in his hand. He once again takes the metallic object and scrapes it across the glass.

"Bradford Andrew Lastings! You cut that out right now young man. You scared mama. And where in the world did you get a fork from."

Brad jumps, he did not expect his mothers sharp tone. The young boy crumples his face, then runs into the living room, fork still in hand. Jennifer chases after him. She takes the fork and again asks where he found it.

"I trying to eat cereal mama. Me got the spoon out of the sink." Brad stares at the floor and starts to pout.

"This", Jennifer says, holding the silverware up in front of her, is a fork honey. Not a spoon. Now get in there to the table and I will get you your breakfast. O.K.?"

Brad shakes his head yes, then scuffs his feet back into the dining room table. He sits up in the chair and impatiently waits for his mother to bring his breakfast.

Jennifer Lastings opens the cupboard next to the stove and removes a box of Lucky Charms. She sets the box on the counter next to the sink while she washes a bowl. A minute later she is pouring the cereal into the clean plastic bowl. She is about to add the milk when the phone rings. She places the milk back in the fridge and quickly runs to the phone. Her heart flutters with excitement as she picks up the phone, hoping for good news. "Hello!"

"Jenny, hey its me. I'm at the mall and I have looked everywhere. She's not here. I mean, I even took a walk inside and found nothing. I'm sorry hon. But she's bound to show up. I'm sure Josie's fine." Derek finds himself on the verge of tears himself.

"My God, what are we gonna do. We have got to find my little girl, we, we just go to." The tears pour out of Jennifer's eyes and again she starts to sob. "I, I don't, I don't know what I'll do if... if somethings happened."

Derek takes a couple deep breaths and tries to get himself under control. "Now just calm down sweetheart. I'm going to find our daughter, don't you worry. Right now, I think we need to catch up with the boy she was last seen with. Ask him when they were last together. And where Josie was when he last seen her."

"U-huh, u-huh, u-huh!" Jennifer continues to cry, she tries to speak, but nothing comes out.

Bradford gets out of his chair and runs to his mother's side. "Why you crying mommy? I sorry I took the spoon."

Jennifer kneels down and pulls Brad into her arms, then hugs him tightly. Derek is quiet on the other end of the phone. He can't seem to find the calming words that he needs so desperately. His heart sinks as he listens to his wife sobbing on the other end of the line. He looks away from the pay phone and to a truck passing out on the main road. "Riley's Carpet and Upholstery" is painted on the side in a teal green. Derek follows the truck up the road until he can no longer see it. A few feet away, an elderly couple exits the mall and steps into the morning sun.

Derek runs his hand from his chin down his neck, then back up again. "Listen, ah, I'm going to come on home to calm you down a little. We'll have a cup a coffee together, then you and I both can go to the police station. Make a report. What do you say?"

Jennifer kisses Brad on the cheek and straightens herself out. She is still a little shaky, but manages to speak. "O.K., um. I'll see you... See you when you get here. O.K. I love you too. Mm, bye bye."

She hangs up the phone then turns back into the kitchen. After pouring the milk, Jennifer carries the bowl of cereal and her son back to the table. She sits Brad back in his seat, then takes one of the chairs next to him.

"Brad, honey, I want you to know that I am not upset with you. Mommy is just a little worried about your sister." Jennifer rubs her sons back and does her best to speak in a slow, soothing voice.

"Josie OK mama, she just at school." Bradford takes another bite of his cereal and smiles at his mom. Jennifer smiles, then, to keep Brad happy, agrees with him.

Michael Lastings awakes to the sunlight shining in his eyes. He looks at the clock, the buzzer rings steady from its speaker. It must have been going off for hours. Michael rubs his eyes and throws the sheets off. After hitting the snooze button, he stumbles his way into the bathroom. As he stands there taking a leak, he runs his hand over the back of his head and finds an over sized goose egg. The night before felt as if it had been weeks ago. The bump on the back of his head proves otherwise though.

Michael had no idea about the situation with Josie, he barely realized what day it is. His alarm clock had read 9:36, two and a half hours after he should have been at work. Now, in nothing but his boxer shorts, Michael lumbers into his small kitchen. As he looks around, he realizes, he had never cleaned up his mess from last night. The milk from the bowl of cereal he threw had now dried on the window. Michael curses out loud, decides against breakfast, and goes into the living room. The mud tracked in still lies in clumps on the floor. The young man shakes his head in frustration as he sits down on the couch and lays his head back. He didn't have a hangover, but the last time he felt like this, him and some buddies had drank far too much and took turns praying to the porcelain Gods.

Michael closes his eyes and wipes a sleepy bug from the corner of his left eye. From the other room, his alarm clock springs back to life.

"Why in the hell didn't I turn that damn thing off?" Michael slowly rises and heads for his bedroom to shut off that hellacious buzzing noise.

Something crashes into the front door. Lastings stares at the front of his house for a moment, then goes to the window. When he sees the person on his front step, Michael forgets all about his headache and races to the front door. When he pulls it open, Josie Lastings falls into his arms.

Chapter 20

Josie dials her brother's number. Michael lived closer to the mall than anyone else she knew and would be able to get there the quickest. No one picks up, the phone rings five, six seven times. No answer. A shadow falls over her! Josie realizes she is trapped and begins to shriek.

Ash reveals his long fangs, they seem to glow inside his mouth. Josie takes another step back and finds her back against a wall. She stops screaming. The thing before her is so dark, its eyes are a piercing black. But it is human. Or at least looks human enough. Ash steps looms even closer to his prey. His hand streaks out, grabbing Josie's hair and pulling her head back to reveal the neck.

This is it, he's going to kill me. He's actually gonna do it. Oh God, Oh God please help.

Josie feels paralyzed under Ash's grip. He has amazing strength. And something else. His hand is cold, even in her hair she can feel the chill from it, like ice. She looks into his face, at the horrid fangs. The fangs that would, in the next moment, be buried deep in her throat. Then, it would be over. Josie clenches the phone even tighter in her hand. She is holding it at her side, and has yet to realize it. But then...

The phone, the phone! I still have it!

Ash leans in closer, going for the girl's jugular. Josie breaks loose of the tightness she had been feeling and swings the phone with deadly force. The ear piece crashes into Ash's mouth, he screams as his left fang shatters. Blood, along with shards of broken tooth spray the wall next to them. Josie drops the phone, hesitates only a moment, and then makes a hasty exit. She runs passed her attacker, down the long corridor of mall and keeps getting it. Ash throws his head back, tasting the blood in his mouth, and smiles. He turns briskly on the heels of his boots, lifting into the air, he takes flight. He charges Josie like a hawk after a scared rabbit. The hare is only yards away and the large bird is quick to catch up. Ash scoops up his prize by the shoulders, then releases as they come over the fountain of water that centers the mall. Josie splashes in and under. She no more and comes up to catch her breath before her attacker drops in on top of her.

Josie struggles to free herself from the tight grasp forcing her under water. She swings all of her limbs back and forth. Fifteen seconds go by, finally the girl finds her head above water again. She inhales half a breath before Ash's hand grasps her throat and prevents any more air to reach her lungs. Josie finds her vision begin to blur, the colorful blocks on the ceiling of the mall blend together.

And it begins to darken. The lights all around her first become brighter, then start to dim by the second. In a desperate attempt to be free, Josie lifts her right leg straight up with all she has left. Ash howls as her knee connects with the crown jewels between his legs. The grip around her neck loosens then falls away as the Ash falls backwards into the water. Lastings fights to catch her breath, unable to move until she does. Once her lung capacity is back to what it should be, she pulls herself out of depths of the fountain. She doesn't look back as her legs take her away from the nightmare behind her. Josie can feel how weak she is from the struggle. A fast walk is all she can muster, and that's pushing it.

A door on the left reads, "Authorized Personnel Only." Josie feels plenty authorized as she pushes her way through, entering a narrow hallway. Dry wall has been hung on either side, the strong smell of plaster lingers in the air. Lastings trudges onward with the feeling she is pulling a small truck behind her. Up ahead, the hallway ends and the area opens up into a large automotive shop.

Sears, she thinks as she looks around. *What a great place to be, and my car has just reached three thousand miles since its last oil change.*

On the opposite side of the wall is a large shelf with a number of tools and parts resting within. To her right is an actual car, a Ford Tempo. Beyond that is the bay doors, and freedom. Yes, freedom.

Something crashes from behind her, she spins around to find Ash has busted through the door she had come from only a minute before. The nocturnal beast lifts to the air once again. He thrusts himself into Josie and they both crash into the concrete floor a few feet in front of them. Lastings finds herself down, but not within the beasts grasp. She struggles to her feet, running for the shelf on the other side of the bay area. Ash's hand grabs her ankle, his sharp nails tear into her pant leg piercing her skin.

Josie screams from the pain, the sound echoes twice before becoming silent again. She turns and kicks his arm away with her other foot and again goes for the large shelf, the one with the tools on it. She finds herself upon it, now what does she grab. A wrench, yes a wrench.

Again the air is knocked out of Josie Lastings as a determined Ash lunges forward and sends the girl stomach first into the one of the shelves. Her hair is moved away and she feels hot breath on her neck as Ash again moves in for the feast. Relentless, Josie swings her elbow back, connecting with his temple. Ash swings in retaliation. The blow catches Lastings on the side of her face and forces her to the floor again. This time her head hits the concrete. Warm blood runs out the back of her head onto the floor.

Ash looks down at his sweet dish. He drops to his knees, straddling the girl then puts his face close to hers. He is so close, Josie can smell his rank breath. His hand falls over her forehead and pushes her head to the side so she is facing the wall. Ash moves to her neck, he doesn't bite right away. He takes his tongue and runs along the length of Josie's neck. This sends a chill down her back, to the rest of her body. She opens her eyes, her head still throbbing from the blow to the concrete. Inches away from her, on the bottom of the shelf lay a tuning fork. Josie eyes it dreamily and grasps it with her left hand.

Ash's teeth puncture her neck, Josie screams and wheels the tool in her hand at her attacker. The fork digs deep into the side of Ash's neck. There is no scream though, Ash goes into an upright position, bolt into it. Blood, dark and purple pours from his neck. It's hot to Josie's skin as it spills from the dark figures cloak onto her.

Ash falls to the floor beside her. Josie feels her eyes water up and the tears stream onto her face. She lifts her hand to her neck, she's bleeding. She isn't sure how bad, only that she aches all over. And her head is pounding. As the girl tries to sit up, she finds little cooperation from the rest of her body. Her mind is sending the message, her body though, isn't receiving it. Or maybe, it ignores it. Minutes pass, several. Josie is sure Ash is going to sit up any second, but he does not.

Lastings touches her neck again, the blood is still coming. She tries to get up again, this time with a little success. The girl gets into a sitting position. She spots a roll of shop towel about eight feet down the shelf. With the help of metal frame beside her, Josie makes it to her feet. Slowly, she baby steps her way to shop towels. She removes two and sticks them in her back pocket. Then two more and presses them firmly to her neck. The pressure hurts, only it doesn't even compare to the throbbing in her head. She looks around again.

OK, the car is still here. And the air is damp. And oil, I can smell the nasty smell of oil in the air. And there, right out that door is freedom.

Josie walks along the side of the shelf, holding on for extra support. The bay door is glass. It has beams running through it about every three feet. If she could break one of the frames of glass, she could get out. Josie stops and looks back at Ash. The tuning fork is still sticking out the side of his neck. She decides against retrieving it, and settles for a crescent wrench instead. She walks over to the bay door and kneels. Her first swing is lazy and weak. The wrench bounces off and nearly flings from her hands. The second, the wrench bursts through. Josie yells in happy success then knocks out the rest of the jagged pieces.

Climbing though the small frame ends up easier than she thought it would be. Hey, at least something has gone right tonight. The air outside is cool, a slight breeze sweeps over the parking lot and suddenly Josie feels down right cold. She looks to the sky and finds the sun is just barely peeking on the horizon. It is still dark though. In a stunning realization, Josie realizes she has been trapped in the mall all night. She had to get home, get to safety.

The highway is vacant for the most part. The occasional car blows by Josie on the right side as she hobbles along side the shoulder. Jose is quickly becoming too weak to walk, the air is cold and the blood running through her veins feels like ice. It seems an eternity goes by, before an oncoming car from the opposite side of the road slows, then stops completely. Lastings does not recognize the car. She couldn't help but go to them though, she had nothing left within to keep her going. Josie crosses the road and approaches the gray Honda Accent ahead. A young gentleman, maybe in his late twenties sits in the driver's seat. He looks nice enough and is dressed in business like attire. He waves his hand for her to get in, she does and the car speeds off into the sunset.

The sun is now fully over the horizon. It shines brightly in the heavens and glistens off the rocky terrain of the mountains edge. A lone figure keeps to the shadows of the mountain, the terrain is very rough, nearly impossible to climb. Seth Wake seems to have no problem at all. On the final ledge before the mountain peaks, Wake stops, he peers into the cave beyond the reach of the sunlight. A full wreath of wild flowers that has no business living on such a surface outlines the entrance to the cave. Etched into a rock on the left is three letters, m-o-m Seth pauses here a moment before entering the darkness, he rubs his hands over the letters and smiles. Certainly not an ordinary smile, one of meaningfulness, one with a plan, evil intentions. He returns to his feet from the crouching position, turns and enters the cave. Along the floor, glowing stones come to life with every step the man takes. Barely enough light to show the way, not that Seth really needs it, he likes them there for his mother though. Wake travels deep onto the bowels of the mountain, nearly three thousand feet.. The path comes to an end. The walls illuminate revealing hundreds of flowers on the walls and floor. And a coffin. The most majestic coffin in existence. The wood is cherry, a brilliant shine comes off the finish. Red velvet lines the top of the eternal resting place. one rose lies on top of it. On the side, the name Alise is written in a perfect gold letters.

Seth allows a tear to roll down his cheek, then wipes it away and again the smile returns.

"Mother, it has been a long time. Too long in fact. But I come with the best of news. Mother, it wont be much longer, no. It wont be much longer and I shall have you again!"

Chapter 21

MICHAEL LASTINGS HELPS HIS sister to the couch. He surveys the damage, the amount of blood stained clothing is alarming. Josie tries to speak, Michael puts a finger to her lips then walks , practically runs into the kitchen. He opens a drawer, finds a washcloth, and then rinses it with cold water. From the fridge, he grabs some ice, and quickly returns to his sister. The cloth he applies to her forehead and the ice he places in her hand. She in turn puts it to the back of her head. Goose bumps rise up on Josie's arms, Michael grabs a blanket from the other side of the couch and lays it over her. She is still quite shaky though, her brother sits down next to her and lets Josie lie her head on his shoulder. A few minutes pass, and finally the girl seems to relax a little. Michael breaks the ice.

"What happened Josie, tell me everything, slowly.

"OK, I will but fist we need to call mom and dad. Or better, take me home, Ok, will tell you on the way." Michael makes his sister rest a few more minutes before they go, on the way she tells him most everything that happened. Naturally, she leaves out the part about making out in the movie theater. The rest she tells pretty good, even the part when she thought she was going to die.

Michael sits silent, intently listening to Josie finish up her story. She is about finished when they pull into their parents drive. Derek's truck is gone. Michael lets Josie sit in the car while he checks if the house is empty. Nobody answers his knocking so he returns to his car. "I guess we wait until they get back. I'm sure they are worried sick. So the best thing we can do is wait. Anyway, tell me the rest. What happened after you stabbed the sun of a bitch and broke your way out? How did you get to my house from the mall?"

Josie still feels tremendous pain, and ponders the thought of asking Michael to carry her to the hospital. Then decides against it. "Well, I went to the road." As Josie speaks, her words are weak. It seems she is having difficulty keeping her breath. "This young gentleman stopped and waved me over. I was scared to death. I didn't recognize the car and had no idea what this guy might have planned for me. But all I could think of was getting away from that monster. So I took my chances. When I got in the car I thought the guy would freak out. The sight of the blood and he said my face had grown quite pale. He insisted I go to the hospital. But I begged him no, to please just take me to my brother's house. Finally he agreed. He asked me so many questions. I just, I just couldn't tell him though. It all seems so crazy, and I am scared Michael. I'm scared to death." The tears start again, Josie starts sobbing like a small child. Michael pulls her head to his shoulder. He doesn't want her to know it, but he has become quite afraid himself. Rage starts to overtake his feelings to the point in which he feels himself begin to shake. He doesnt let it consume him though. He has to remain calm for his sister. After a few deep breaths, the anger passes.

"I ah, I cant imagine the pain and the fear you are feeling now sis. I know you must feel like you will go crazy. I wont let them get you. I'm by your side till this thing is over. From here on out Josie, those motherfuckers will have to come through me to get to you. I'm gonna take care of you sis, just like I always have."

Josie calms a little, the sobbing slows, the tears still roll from her eyes though. She tries to gather herself. To think of something other than the horror she feels now. Her brother's words have a lot of meaning. He really has been there for her. A few years back he had helped her out of a bad situation with an ex-boyfriend. The guy had had an obsession with her. When she broke it off, Telley just could not let it go. It started with letters and phone calls begging her back. It only got worse from there. He would follow her down the halls at school. Or show up unannounced at the front door. On one occasion he did this, only Josie was home. The times before, Derek had run the boy off. This time when Josie answered the door, Telley forced his way in. He looked at the phone and started yelling at her. Asking who the hell she was talking to, and why did things have to be this way. Telley tore the phone from her hand and dropped it on the floor. Josie backed away from him. He kept yelling, and began pushing her. This went on for several minutes, him demanding answers and telling her that she needed him. Josie went to pull away again and Telley grabbed her by the arm. When she slapped him with her free hand, the boy hit her back. Hit her open handed right across the face. She stumbled back and almost went down. She didn't though, she forced herself to stay up. Telley pushed her again, this time the back of her legs hit the couch and she spilled backwards. He falls on top of her. Josie remembers being scared then too, scared of what this guy might do to her. Telley took hold of both her hands and starts to kiss her lips. The weight of his body keeps her legs pinned to the couch. He releases her arms and grabs her breasts with both hands. His grip is hard enough to hurt. Josie starts to pound on his back, only it seems not to bother him. Then, in busts Michael like ol John Wayne. Telley pops up from on top of Josie and meets a left fist with his face. The two go at each other for a minute until finally Michael wraps both his arms around Telley and forces him back against the wall. The force of it knocks the breath right out of him. Mike connected with a few more lefts to the head and then threw the boy out on the porch. To this day, Josie still joked with him on how he came busting in like the Duke.

"So does that mean your gonna break out the boots, the spurs and the cowboy hat Mr. Wayne?" Josie does her best to give a smile and a small laugh. Michael laughs

a little. He is about to reply when they hear dad's old truck pull in behind them. Jennifer jumps out of the passenger seat and runs to Michael's car. Upon seeing Josie with him, she again lets the tears fall as she opens the door and sweeps her precious daughter into her arms. Josie cries with her. Her mom holds her for quite some time before releasing her and taking a good look. She gasps at the sight of the blood on her little girl's neck. Michael starts to explain what exactly happened as his father stands silent. He gives his sons words full attention. A few seconds later Brad becomes restless sitting in the truck and makes his way out. He runs to his mother and big sister and hugs them both. Several minutes later, when all have regained their composure, Josie is finally taken to the hospital.

The Mays house is left empty, Sandra and Eric have gone out for the evening. Nothing fancy, just dinner and then a ride around the city. They had to just get away, if only for a little while. This leaves Lisa and Tommy the house to themselves. Lisa leads her boyfriend down a long hall and into her bedroom where she shuts and locks the door behind them. She has him sit on the side of the bed, the pushes him to his back. Tommy watches on as she lifts her shirt over her head and tosses is to the floor. "Are you sure you want to do this baby, Tommy begins, I mean with Josie missing and all?"

"Josie is my best friend baby, but I'm sure she is just fine. She likely is doing the exact thing were about to do with her little crush right now." Lisa reaches back and unhooks her bra, lets it fall to the floor. "Besides, can you think of a better way to relieve all the stress in the air?"

Tommy eyes his luscious treat dreamily, he reaches for her and she moves to him. He pulls her gently on top of him and kisses her deeply. The couple continues to shed each other's clothing until their hands can run freely over the others bare-naked body. They give each other great pleasure for the better part of an hour. And then, they lay motionless next to one another, staring into each other's eyes, and for the moment, giving each other a small feeling of security. Only, it would not last. As the two lovers lay there, looking at the other, something changes in Tommy's eyes. They slowly go from a look of love and lust to a look of horror. Lisa is startled by the fright in her boyfriend's eyes and face. She wants to look behind her, wants to see what it is that Tommy sees. But she can't bring herself to do it. There's someone in the room with them, or something. Lisa starts to shake as the fear overwhelms her. She wants to scream, to ask what's wrong with him. Only she doesn't really, deep down want to know at all.

Tommy's eyes are open, but what he is seeing isn't in the room, or even happening at all. No, it's not a memory, at least, not one of his own. He sees the woman from the book that Josie had shared with them all. Alise, the vampire witch. The one that Joseph Critton had killed. She appears to be dead, her eyes open, staring directly at Tommy. She is lying in a coffin, and her arms begin to twitch. They slowly reach out, motioning to Tommy. Like she is beckoning him to come closer. To his horror, he does go closer. He doesn't want to, though it seems the decision is not his to make. The temperature drops, the woman's eyes blacken. Alise opens her mouth to speak. The words are softly spoken yet loud and very clear in Tommy Critton's mind. "Your uncle didn't finish the job Tommy. I am only resting. Soon I will rise again, and it shall be you who will pay for the sins of your descendant."

As sudden as the image appeared, it is now withdrawn. Tommy screams as he snaps back into reality. It's cold, freezing. Lisa jumps to her feet, screaming as well. She backs away and watches her boyfriend sit up. He puts his hands in his face, and for the very first time in front of Lisa, he cries.

Dale Sanders looks out and over the hill in his three quarter acre back yard. He can already see the outline of the moon in the sky. A few seconds pass, the wind blows through his hair, a dog barks in the distance. Dale decides he has had enough for one day, the yard is about done and he has become quite tired from landscaping all day. He walks idly to the back of his house. The TV is on in the living room. Dale can see it though the double sliding doors as he walks across his back patio. At this point of view, you can look right through the kitchen and passed the doorway leading to the living room. Upon entering the house, he wipes his feet on the mat to avoid unnecessary dirt in his kitchen floor. Dale did not mind getting dirty himself, but he is the quite the neat freak when it comes to his house. After all, the man had worked the last ten years of his life for the luxury of his own home. And made sure to take care of his investment. The news is on the television. He listens to the reporter as he prepares himself a tall glass of cold milk.

...and if that was not already enough to keep you awake at night, it only gets worse. Two high school students were found dead today. One of the boys met his demise from lacerations to the neck. The other young man was found with a crushed skull and a broken neck. The police once again have no leads and earlier when asked what they planned to do about the apparent situation at hand...well, there would be no comment. Very disturbing if you ask this news journalist. A killer on the loose, and the police at a loss. The citizens of Trench are looking for answers and are getting nothing in return. How long will this go on, is anybody safe? And do the authorities have the means to stop this madness? All these questions we hope to answer in the days to come. That's all for now. Back to you Joan...

Dale picks up the remote and hits the power button, the TV falls silent. He speaks out loud to the empty house, mockingly, "A killer on the loose and the police at a loss. Back to you Joan." He chuckles and takes another sip of milk. The quiet still of the house echoes through his ears. The silence in the air is calming, yet calamitous. Dale sits down in his easy chair, lays his head back and thinks of the next days work. His eyes become heavy, and as the sky continues to darken outside, Dale Sanders falls into his eternal sleep. Ambrose looks down on his lifeless body from behind the chair. He brings his knife from Dales neck to his lips. And though the search would not end hear, the blood is warm and fresh. Ambrose sheaths his knife and now prepares to feast on the fallen pray before him.

Chapter 22

The morning air is cool, almost brisk as it sweeps along the mountainside. The sun is just now stretching its long arms out over the dark and damp countryside. A figure climbs his way to a hole in the side of the mountain. He reaches the cave entrance and is immediately met by his brother. Ash brings himself to a full standing position. There is no sign of struggle from two nights before. His wounds have completely healed over. His strength is at its fullest, and it seems as if ten years has been taking from his physical appearance. Seth looks into his brother's eyes and smiles, then greets him with a long embrace. They release moments later, Seth places a cigarette between his lips. The force of the wind seems non-existent as he lights the end of the tobacco. For the flame does not even waver as Seth strikes his lighter. "Our search ends then. Congratulations my brother, you have found the one we have been seeking. Why has Ambrose not joined us here?"

Ash looks passed Seth to the cave behind him, "I knew where to find you because I had reason to do so. For Ambrose, the search is still ongoing. Remember Seth, we do not have same powers in which you posses. I knew as soon as you seen me you would know, that you would be able to see within me. And better, see the one who will save our father. I do not know her, only if I seen her again. So our search is only three quarters of the way done brother. I think it best that you summon Ambrose, let him know we have found the one...

"Pardon the interruption, but I know of this one. Her name is Josie Lastings, and tracking her will be simple. Ambrose will meet us at the valley, and from there, we will take what is ours." Seth takes another drag off his cigarette and flicks it to the winds. He steps to the edge of the mountainside, Ash's hand grasps his shoulder.

"Seth, show me your mothers resting place. You have always forbid us to enter. I'm asking you to share it with me." He releases his hand from his brother's shoulder, Seth turns to him.

His face is cold, his eyes black. "Ash, my brother. I share in my fathers love for you. In my eyes you are nothing less than my brother. But I will not share my mother with you. And if you should decide to enter her tomb alone, I will know about it. And I promise you this, the only way you will leave it will be as a dead, stinking corpse." Seth turns his back to Ash once again, stepping to the edge of the mountainside. "Now, let us be off to the valley. So we may share our news with Ambrose." And Seth steps off the edge. His form wavers, the wind catches wings. A black bat takes to the skies. Another follows only seconds after.

Josie Lastings is treated and kept overnight for observation. She is released to leave at eleven o'clock the next day. Its Monday morning, she would not return to school that week. Michael has chosen to stay with her. He calls his boss that morning to explain what happened. And that he would be out for a few days. Eric Mays is very understanding and says he will pass the news on to Lisa and Tommy. Josie is happy to ride home with her brother. After all, there is no way the whole family can fit into Derek's old truck. On the way to the hospital, Josie had rode with her mom and dad. Michael carried Brad along in his car. Michael gets the door for Josie then closes it behind her once he is sure she is in and comfortable. His plans are to stay by her side no matter what. They pull out of the hospital parking deck and head down highway 90. That would carry them back to the border of Trench and from there they would take a few back roads to shorten the trip back to the house. Derek follows close behind in his pickup. Michael reaches for the radio, he cant stand driving without his tunes. He pauses right before hitting the power button. "The Valley" The words come to him softly in his head. "Ambrose, meet us in The Valley." Yes, that was it. The voice in his head belonged to none other than Seth Wake. Somehow, Michael could hear him calling to his brother. The pure thought of this spooks him, but at the same time, he feels like he could use this to his advantage. He puts these thoughts aside for now and turns on the radio. He plays it loud enough to hear clearly, but low enough not to hurt his sister's head. Josie falls asleep on the way home. Michael's glad, she can use all the rest she can get. The car holds a solid sixty-five. A couple cars to the left of him pass by, and then a tractor trailer. He can remember how at a younger age the size of those things made him very nervous. That had gone away over the years and for that, Michael is thankful.

A little ways back, Derek holds the steering wheel steady. Brad is next to him. It wont be long and the young boy will be in the same state as his older sister, fast asleep.

Jennifer sits silent, staring out the window. The thoughts going through her head are harsh and unpleasant. It seems to her that a giant hand has grabbed the city and is squeezing it into submission. Dark clouds of fear have moved in and consumed the residents, herself included. She understands that things could have gone bad here, very bad. Her little girl, seventeen or not, she would always be Jennifer's little girl in her eyes, was almost taking from her. And that scared her more than anything. Too many had perished already. She prays quietly to herself that no more would. As the family draws closer to the city of Trench, the trees begin to thicken. They grow closer together and the sparsely spread trees soon become the forest. As they cross the border of Spontania and enter their hometown, a lake comes into view just up the road on the right. Trees cover the land around it. The lake is rather large. A few dead trees even stand within it. This is the same lake spoke of in the book Josie had borrowed from the library, Before Trench City. After the lake comes more trees. Then a bearing valley. And once again the thick and over grown forest for which the city is mostly known for. Jennifer turns away from the window and peers at her husband. She stays this way until...

Michael turns the radio tuner in an attempt to find something a little more upbeat. Instead of music, a voice comes from his speakers. "Welcome back to the city Michael. It's no secret I know where you live, and in only a few minutes you will take me to where Josie is staying. I can see everything you see Michael. If you're lucky, my brothers and I will stop in for a cup of tea. Now doesn't that sound nice." Michael hits the power button, the voice is gone, Seth is gone. Michael suddenly hits the breaks, pulling to the side of the road. Behind him, his father does the same.

Derek looks on bewildered as Michael gets out of the car and jogs toward the truck. "Dad, dad! They know where we are going. Were leading them right to us. I mean I am leading them right to us."

"What? What are you talking about son. Well be safe at the house. All of us together...

"No dad. You don't understand. He wants Josie, they want Josie." Michael's words come as desperate and pleading.

Jennifer speaks up before Derek has the chance to reply. "Who Michael? Who is they, and why would they want Josie?"

"Just trust me, I mean isn't it obvious. We just left the hospital for Christ sake because one of Seth's brothers attacked her. And now all three will come. You have to listen to me. Come on mom, dad, I'm not making this up. These guys are dangerous. They've already killed half a dozen people, maybe more. Don't you see, we can't go home."

Derek shakes his head at looks at Jennifer, then back to his son. "Look Michael, I have guns at the house. We can call the police and tell them we have reason to believe that we could be in danger. I am not gonna let anything happen to...

"We can't stop them dad, we cant."

Brad opens his eyes and starts crying, "Momma, why is daddy and Mitle yelling?"

Derek pats him on the head, "Everything is fine boy, just chit chat." He turns back to Michael. "Were going home now." Michael drops his head, looking at the gravel-covered ground below him. He starts to speak again, only to be cut off by Derek. "Michael!" I said were going home."

Frustrated, Michael realizes his fight is futile. He trudges back to his car and hops in. Josie has not moved, she is still sleeping soundly. Both vehicles move back onto the road and back up to speed. Fifteen minutes later, they arrive home.

Once the family is in the house and settled, Josie in her own bed, and Brad asleep on the couch; Michael explains he needs to run home for a minute. As he exits the house, Jennifer and Derek have settled in at the dining room table for coffee. Michael speeds away in the direction of his own home. The mustang reaches speeds of eighty miles an hour then up to ninety. He arrives home in only a few minutes. The car door swings shut behind him, the front door of the house is left wide open. His line of thinking is simple. To retrieve his bow from the closet, load up on arrows, find his hunting knife and head for the valley. Michael knows this is not the brightest idea in the world. But he would be the first to say, sometimes he was more brave than he was smart. It turns out his knife is buried in with his fishing tackle. He pushes aside a few weights and fishing lures, pulls his knife from within, sticks it in his pocket. Then, the oldest of the Lastings offspring sets off to face what had to be certain death. Though he would likely fail, and chances were pretty slim that he would be the hero of the day, he had to try. Michael Lastings had to at least try and keep these killers from his parent's house, no matter the cost.

The High school is open, only, the amount of students attending class is considerably less than usual. The halls have not been this empty since the last senior skip day. And even then, it was not this bad. The city of Trench has been gripped with fear. Parents have come to a point where they are afraid to let their children out of the house. Tommy Critton and Lisa Mays did make it. They walk down the hall holding hands, boyfriend and girlfriend trudging on to the next class. They do know Josie's situation, they know she had been attacked and would be okay. The two young lovers are quite afraid themselves, especially with the events of the night before. Tommy had had a very strange image, or dream, or whatever the hell and it had really scared Lisa. They do not know what to make of it, what it means, or how much trouble they are actually in.

"I guess your dad is gonna be a little short at work until Michael comes back. He is one of his best workers." Tommy does his best to make small talk as he walks Lisa to her next class. He doesn't want to think about the events of the past couple weeks, so he brings up other subjects in an attempt to give his lover a normal feel on things.

"Huh, oh! Well he'll just work with them like he usually does, besides, he still has Kenny, Dale, and Timothy. What makes you bring that up anyway? We never talk about my dads work."

"Just making conversation hon, oh well. Hey I was thinking we could grab a burger after school, then go see how Josie is doing."

Lisa stops, turns to Tommy. They stop only a few steps from her next class. "Why all of a sudden do you have this urge to talk about Josie all the time. I mean, is it because she has bigger boobs or something? Or maybe you just think it would feel good to have those pretty poutty lips wrapped around your...

"Lisa," Tommy calls her name loud enough for another student just up the hall to over hear, the student cuts her eyes at him. "Where is this coming from, Josie's your best friend, I thought you would be worried and maybe want to check in on her. So I thought I would make a suggestion. I'm not attracted to Josie Lastings all right, and... You know what, forget it? I'm not even gonna try and defend myself to you. Just forget I said anything."

Lisa giggles, "So, are you done yet?" Tommy is flabbergasted by her actions. Now she's giggling. "Good! I got you. Sounds like a great idea babe, see you after science." Lisa gives Tommy a quick kiss on the cheek, then trots off into class. Tommy stands in his exact spot for about twenty seconds. He finally smiles and begins to shake his head. Under his breath, he speaks aloud to himself. "Oh

Lisa Mays, your gonna pay for that one." He laughs a little himself as he proceeds on to his own class.

Steven Mass and Matthew Turry pull up in front of Michaels place. They had not seen him in awhile and thought they would visit. It quickly becomes apparent, they're good buddy isn't home. They assume him to be at work. After all, didn't everybody work on Mondays? Well, except for them of course. Steven mostly works Wednesday through Saturday at a small mechanic and repair shop in Spontania. Matthew on the other hand is between jobs. Steven looks at his watch as he closes the driver side door. "Well, I reckon we could get a bite to eat. Its almost noon. What do you say?" Only, when he says this, it comes out more like, "Whadoyasay?"

Matthew turns his head from the passenger side window to look at his friend. As he does he winces a bit. The night before he had fallen asleep in the chair watching television. It made for a bad nights sleep and one hell of a kink in his neck. "Well, food sounds purty good. But I tell you what, I sure can go for an ice cold drink. My mouth is so fucking dry and hot I fear my hair may catch on fire every time I exhale."

Steven laughs, "You know, I just don't see myself getting that lucky." Both laugh, and Steven pulls away from Michaels house headed for the Trench-Spontania border. McDonald's is calling his name.

The forest is every bit as thick as Michael remembers it from the last time he made this journey. He can find his way though. As before, he can feel his way through it. The young man carries his bow along with a dozen arrows, in the bag in witch they came, slung over his shoulder. His knife is tucked away in the back pocket of his jeans. And he carries a Springfield 22 rifle in his left hand. His dad had bought him this a few years ago for his birthday. Michael keeps it hidden in his trunk under the carpet, it doesn't leave that spot. Unless of course, he is cleaning it, or hunting. In a way, Michael feels he is hunting. Hunting the dark beast that must be slain in order to protect the fair maiden. In this case, his very own sister. Could it be though, could it be he is hunting an animal in which he cannot kill. The answer would come soon enough. He comes to the clearing him and Steven had come to the other night. That meant a couple of things to him. One, he is indeed onto the right track, not that he ever doubted it. And the other, he is making much better time on this go round. The valley in which he seeks would be only a few more hundred yards. What an idea this was, one man on his way two face three. Three what? Well, they're not exactly poster children for the American Idle Award. Their monsters. No other way to put it than that. Cold, calculated, and deadly. And in just a couple more minutes, he, Michael Lastings would be in the din of the wolf. Perhaps coming here was not the most pragmatic decision he could have made, but he could not regress now.

Michael slows himself, takes heed in his actions. He must move silently now. Three beings come into view as he gazes out across the valley. Their shadows stretch the length of the grounds. Sort of like in those old country western movies. The gunfighters moving in as the sun casts a lone obscuration over the dusty terrain. Seth stands before his two brothers speaking what seems to be silent words. Its like he is the general, and his brothers are two privates taking orders from there superior.

Michael perceives them to be about two hundred yards away. He could take a shot from this distance with substantial accuracy, only, if he could get about twenty to twenty five yards closer; well all the better. Michael is prudent with his movements as he proceeds through the brush along the edge of the valley. He knows there is a good chance that Seth Wake already knows he is there. In fact, he is quite sure of it. As the young man makes his post, he lifts the rifle to his shoulder. Seth is the one he wants, the one he aches to kill, though, for reasons even he is unsure of himself, it is Ambrose he finds in his sites. Michael moves from neck to head several times wondering which would do the worst. It will be the neck he takes a shot at. The gun is steady, his finger on the trigger. All it would take is a little more pressure on the trigger. Michael lets a feeling of guilt wash over him. He starts telling himself he can't do it. That he wont. A second before he can convince himself otherwise, Michael squeezes the trigger, the gun fires.

Chapter 23

JOSIE LASTINGS LAY SILENT and peaceful in her bed. The young girl has been through quite an ordeal. Now she dreams of her big crush Craig Johnson. Her thoughts had turned a little to James Smilot, but after the other night with Craig things were different. Even with all the hell she felt after their little date, it is still him in her dreams. The couple is walking across a bridge made of wood. A beautiful clear stream runs beneath it. The birds are chirping, and Josie can even feel a warm breeze on her skin. The feel of it all forces her to believe it is reality. After all, no dream could feel this real. Craig is holding her hand, he seems to be leading her somewhere. They're talking and laughing. Both are wearing swimsuits. Josie, a two piece bikini, red and very revealing. Craig in a pair of black trunks. From the bridge, the couple steps onto a gravel path. The rocks seem to crunch under each step, only they never hurt her feet. Off to the right are two beautiful statues that stand at least five feet. One is a beautiful woman with wings, and you can almost see a glow coming off her face. That is probably just the one the sun is positioned though.

The other statue is a handsome man, with horns and a spike tail. Josie perceives it to be the little devil chasing an angel. Or maybe, a man with indecent thoughts after the woman he met earlier that day. Between the statues starts a narrow dirt path. Craig Johnson leads her right this way. Josie runs her hand over the statue of the woman as they step off the gravel and onto the earth. The little devil leads his very own angel down this winding path. Every tree along the way looks to be spaced perfectly, like soldiers lining up for role call. About a quarter mile of walking takes them to the banks of the stream and a pair of steps. The stone steps feel cool beneath her bare feet. At the bottom of the stair is a quaint little spot, tucked just under the bridge, and out of sight. A blanket has been spread a few feet away from one of the main supports for the bridge. On this she finds their names. Craig pulls Josie into his arms, he presses his lips to her own. The feeling that follows is one that she could almost float away, the real world is non-existent.

The grandfather clock in the living room chimes one o'clock. Derek Lastings glances at it from the couch where he sits with his wife's head on his shoulder. He has her lean up so he may stand. Derek takes his coffee cup from the table and walks into the kitchen. He steps with a slight limp, his left leg asleep. The pins and needles are there every step of the way. He crosses the kitchen to the coffee maker and pours what is left into his cup. He puts on another pot, then decides to check in on Josie while he waits for it to brew. He stops to straighten a family portrait on his way down the hallway. The Lastings had always used these walls for special family moments caught on camera. Derek comes to Josie's door. In an attempt not to wake or disturb her, Derek doesn't knock but enters slowly. As he looks over her, he finds a smile on her face. He is pleased to see her resting peacefully, and thanks God her dreams are pleasant and not of the horror she had experienced two nights before. Satisfied, Derek goes back to the kitchen to finish his coffee, then once again joins Jennifer on the couch. Little Brad Lastings rests his head on his mama's lap, and mom rests her head on dads shoulder. For the moment things are ok, right as rain.

Seth pauses halfway through his sentence, it's only for a moment though. He knows of the threat stalking them only a couple hundred yards away. Ash and Ambrose pay close attention as Seth continues his words. The wind picks up as it flows across the valley. A group of birds fly off, spooked by the sudden change in the air. A shot rings out of the thick forest. The bullet rips through the left jugular vein of Ambrose's neck. Dark blood, almost purple squirts in increments from the wound as Ambrose falls to the ground of the valley. Seth does not even blink. Ash spins around looking wildly for the source. Two more shots come, one right after another. One breezes by Ash's left ear. The other pierces the skin of his right shoulder and embeds itself in his shoulder blade. The wound hurts, but Ash is relentless. He takes to all fours, his head becomes misshapen, his legs and arms shrink up. White hair explodes form every part of his body. Within seconds, there is a white wolf in place of the man that stood before. Two more shots come slicing out through the forest green. Both miss Seth Wake by inches, it's as if they take a curve ball effect in mid-air. This goes unnoticed by the naked eye, but occurs just the same. Seth still stands his ground, his eyes glazed over as if he has gone into some sort of trance. The white wolf continues to close in on the source of the gunfire.

Michael Lastings lowers his aim to the animal charging him, it only about fifty yards now. He still has plenty of ammo, ten, eleven shots left before he would be empty. The gun would hold sixteen rounds. Lastings though, could not remember if he had fired five or six. No time to think now though. Three more rounds are fired. One appears to hit the wolf square in the face, the other two go astray. Yes, it would be a direct hit. The head of the white wolf turns red in the matter of seconds. It slows considerably from the shot, but somehow keeps coming. Michael wants to look away from the wolf, see what affect his first shot had on Ambrose. More than that, he wants to know if Seth has turned his attention this way or not. No mistakes, he has to keep his head. It is going better than he had originally thought and he couldn't fuck it up now. He takes aim again, the target moving at half the speed it was only seconds before. He fires.

The white wolf stops dead in its tracks then drops in a heap on the ground. "Seth, I do believe I just sunk your battle ship." Michael chuckles at himself. He looks back to Seth and Ambrose. Ambrose is up to one knee, his hand clinching his neck. The flow of blood is still considerable. Michael had taken one hell of a shot. Seth on the other hand has indeed turned his attention to Michael. His eyes seem to be locked right on him. Michael raises his rifle again. *Come on you son of a bitch, keep coming!* And Seth does keep coming, stalking towards Michael Lastings.

The gun fires again, followed by two then three more after. None meet their mark. The fear begins to creep up Michaels back. It's as if he can't hit him. Two more rounds blast out of the barrel of the Springfield twenty-two. Once again they change direction, going two or three inches to either side of Seth.

The gun locks up, Michael squeezes the trigger and nothing happens. Seth is quickly putting less ground between the two of them. He drops the gun and reaches for his bow. The zipper on the bag sticks for a moment before Lastings can remove the weapon. Finally, Michael stands, pulls the bow back as far as he can and lets the arrow fly. Time seems to stand still. The arrow is in slow motion. It is dead on with Seth Wake's heart. It doesn't waiver or turn. Victory starts to sweep in, where the fear has now gone. Michael looks on, hoping, praying for the point of the arrow to punch right through the chest of Seth, and puncture the heart.

Seth Wake reaches out and catches the arrow with his bare hands. Michael looks on with mixed emotions of shock, fear, and bewilderment. He reaches for another arrow, fumbles it and drops it into the green shrubs below. He goes for another. Wake is upon him, his hand grabs Michaels throat. He is lifted into the air almost two feet from the ground, the air cramps in his lungs. Michael tries to swing his legs out, kick his attacker, anything to make him let lose. It is not to be. Seth Wake holds him this way almost to the point of blacking out, then drops him. Michael gasps for air, his lungs and throat burn. His vision is blurry, but he can see the outline of Death before him. And that's exactly what he believed it to be. No, it's not Seth Wake standing over him, at least, not alone. The Reaper has joined him, the Grim one has come to take him to whatever comes after your earthly life. He speaks.

"Michael, I'm flattered you would come all this way just to kill my brothers and I. You deserve the Purple Heart. Isn't it funny how ninety percent of the ones that receive that honor are already dead. Don't worry, you will soon join them. Not yet though. No, that pleasure I will give to my dear Ash and Ambrose." Seth's voice changes from cool and calm to harsh and hateful. It booms in Michael's ears, Seth is almost screaming. "Damn it Lastings, I had other plans for you. Big plans Michael. You've ruined that now, ruined it. You know Michael Lastings, I tend not to anger easily. But you really fucked things up, and you will suffer. You were supposed to be the lifeblood to bring back my mother. Your life, my powers. It would have been perfect Michael." Seth's voice lowers again, back to calm and cool. "You were gonna wash while I dried Michael Lastings. I the hand, and you the glove. It only puts things off a bit though. Once we have your sister's blood, all will be well. My father will come to full strength and with him my mother can live again. You see, its nothing personal Michael. We just need what your sister has. And that is the rarest blood type in the world. Once every three hundred years Michael Lastings. That makes Josie something special doesn't it?"

Michael works to get to his elbows. His vision has returned to normal and he has regained most of his wits. Seth steps toward him, Michael grabs the knife from his pocket, in one motion opens it and thrusts it at Seth. His reflexes are too much. Seth grabs Michael's hand before the knife can do any damage. Then he gives it a quick twist, shattering the bones in his wrist. Lastings screams in pain. Seth kicks him in the chest, and then begins to drag him into the valley towards his brothers. Ash has returned to human form, but is still motionless. His face is a bloody mess, one of his ears hang from a strand of flesh. Ambrose has made it to his feet. He walks slowly in the direction of Seth and Michael, hand still pressed firm against his neck. Seth stops at Ash's deathly still body, and drops Michael beside him. "Feast my brother, have your fill."

The pain that Michael feels is immense. He knows he has to get passed it though, if not, this would be his end. Determined to stay alive, Michael makes one last attempt to escape his demise. With the help of his good arm, Michael almost jumps to his feet. He swings wildly at Wakes head. Again Seth catches his hand, or fist, and this time turns it behind his back. A basic wrestling hold if you will. What he does next is enough to take any fight Michael Lastings has left in him, completely out. Seth takes the heel of his boot and kicks Michael in the side of the knee, completely dislocating his kneecap and tearing any and all muscle tissue within. An earth-shattering scream echoes through out the vast emptiness of the valley. Once again, Michael falls helpless to the ground. He drops like a shot from a gun. A Springfield-22 if you will. Tears stream down his face, he continues to moan as the inundating pain ravages his entire body. Seth steps back, glaring down at his fallen prey. "Well Michael, dinner is served my friend. And your blood happens to be the main course. Like I said before, nothing personal."

Ash raises his upper body, crawls slowly over to Michael. The pain the young adult is going through is so excruciating, he can feel the lights going out. He manages a few words between grunts and groans. "Please, I... Please don't! I don't w-want to die. Please, p-please don't... kill...me..."

A bead of sweat rolls off the young teenagers forehead. The perspiration comes as her dream not only heats up, but begins to sizzle. Josie Lastings is lying back on the blanket with Craig Johnson on top of her. His tongue enters her mouth as he slides her bathing suit bottoms down her thighs. She had already removed her top moments before. Josie runs her hands down her lovers back, takes hold of his trunks and slides them down as well. She knows she is about to partake in the greatest pleasure she has ever felt. She tries to keep from shaking in anticipation, only it is no use. She moans as Craig's hardness presses against her. Her body feels as if it will explode, Josie cant wait for what comes next.

A shadow falls over the two lovers. It goes unnoticed at first. Then a hand grabs Craig Johnson by the hair and yanks him from his intimate position. The young man falls back on the dirty terrain below him. Josie freezes in sheer horror as she watches Ash move over to him. His boot is placed on the neck of her teenage crush, her lover, her dear Craig Johnson. She wants to scream, but nothing comes out. Wants to run, but cant move. A sound, so sickening it would make any man quiver, comes from Craig's throat as Ash crushes his Adams apple with his boot. Now he turns to her, Craig Johnson's dying blood curdled moans coming form behind him. Josie finds the strength to pull herself back on her elbows. *No, No, please God no. Leave me alone.* Ash's body falls on top of her, she is rendered helpless. He speaks to her. *I had to come back for another taste, the first was so sweet.* Josie can do little as her head is shoved to the side. Ash bears his teeth and prepares to tear the throat out of the young vixen.

A scream rips through the Lastings' house as Josie sits bolt up in her bed. She screams a second time. And begins to yell. "No! No! Oh God, No!" Derek bursts though the door and runs over to his scared and shaken daughter. Jennifer is close behind. From the other room, Brad starts to cry. The house that was filled with good and descent thoughts minutes before, is blown to hell once again. Josie loses it. She sobs like a small child on her fathers shoulder.

The final bell rings at Trench City High School. The students that attended school on this day, only a little more than half, rush to their lockers. Tommy pushes the exit door open and walks out onto the student parking lot. The cool wind hits his face. It feels good against his skin, his final period always seemed to feel like a sauna. Tommy stops at the beginning of the blacktop to wait for his sweet heart. He takes the keys from his pocket and twirls it around his pointer finger for a second. A few students rush by him. "Hey Tommy," a voice says as they pass by. He looks over just in time to see Lindsey Boggs wink at him, then give a small giggle. Tommy waves and smiles. He has known that one for quite some time. About six or seven years. She has had a crush on him for the last three. Tommy watches her walk away, shaking her butt every step of the way. "Like what you see, Mr. Critton?"

Tommy jumps at the voice from behind him, its Lisa. He turns to her. "Not as much as the one I behold before me now. So ah, how was your last two classes?"

Lisa gives Tommy a small look of jealousy, but does not pursue it. "Well, you know. Too much like schoolwork. But, Craig Johnson smiled at me in seventh period."

Tommy rolls his eyes, puts his arm around Lisa's waist as they start toward the car. "Is that right? Well I guess your panties are all wet now, aren't they? Shoot Lis, I think you could do better than that if you were trying to make me jealous. I mean, Craig is Josie's little crush. You aint gonna step on her toes."

Lisa laughs, "You right baby, speaking of Josie, we still going to see her. I want to see how bad that monster messed her up."

"I think I will just drop you off. I mean, I don't know if I could keep my eyes off those big tits of hers long enough to have a conversation. And besides, my girl might get jealous if I go over there."

"Oh stop it," Lisa slaps her boyfriend playfully on the shoulder. "You know I was just playing with you. So are we going or not?"

Tommy unlocks the passenger side door of his car and opens it. "Sure babe, whatever you like." A hand falls on Tommy's shoulder. He spins around, slightly startled. A tall man, a little ragged looking in the face looks back at him. He's wearing a black duster, his hair in a ponytail. And he's holding something in his right hand.

"Hello Tommy. The name is Sage. You don't know me, but rest assured, I know you. No, no don't be nervous, I'm a friend. That may be a tad bit hard to swallow with all that is going on, me being a stranger and all. But trust me young Critton, I'm on your side." The man sticks his hand out to shake Tommy's hand, Lisa protests.

"Get in the car Tommy, please. I'm scared, we don't know this guy, and I don't think I want to."

Tommy steps back, closes the car door and looks the man up and down. "You have a lot of nerve man. I aint sticking around to find out what's going on here. Or even to find out how the hell you know my name." Tommy turns his back, walks to the other side of the car. Lisa unlocks his door for him. He takes one last glance at Sage before he opens his door and prepares to get in.

Sage runs his fingers through his hair, then pulls a pack of Winston's from his coat pocket. "If you wont listen to me Tommy, at least listen to one of your own, Joseph Critton." The man with the ponytail, ragged goatee and duster slides the small, worn black bag across the hood of Tommy's car. Tommy looks at it, hard. Then looks back to the stranger, Sage.

"Don't... kill... me..." Michael Lastings body shuts down, he passes out just as he gets the last word out. Blood from Ash's mutilated face falls on Michael's chest. He leans down and buries his teeth in the neck of Josie's older brother, and he feeds. Ambrose drops to his knees as he waits his turn. Seth places a cigarette between his lips, lights it. The flame continues to burn even after the tobacco is lit. Seth takes his knife from its sheath. He runs his tongue down the length of the knife. Now he puts the flame to it. The blade erupts into a fireball. It burns long enough to leave the blade red hot. Seth takes a step closer to Ambrose, pulls his hand away from his neck, and places the side of the knife firmly against the wound. Ambrose winces in terrible anguish, but holds in the pain as much as possible. When the red-hot knife is removed, the wound is closed, and the bleeding has stopped. Seth puts his knife away, turns away from his brothers, and looks out to the road about a half-mile out. A buzzard is doing some feeding of its own at the side of the highway. Some unsuspecting deer had apparently tried to cross and been mauled by an oncoming vehicle. A cool breeze blows through Seth Wake's hair. He takes another drag from his cigarette. "Its ashame young Lastings. It in fact, is a Goddamn Greek tragedy. Your memory will remain burned in the pits of my mind. Rest in Piece Michael Dwayne Lastings, Ashes to ashes, and dust to dust."

Chapter 24

ONLY A FEW SELECT vehicles remain in the school parking lot. The ones that belong to the big time Varsity Basket ball guys, some teachers, and Tommy Critton. Lisa, Tommy, and this guy that has seemingly popped up out of thin air, Sage, sit on the curb at the rear of the parking lot. Sage has given Tommy a very old journal, it belonged to his distant grandfather. About four generations before him. That grandfather's name was Joseph Critton. Tommy and Lisa are still unsure of this Sage, but they have come to trust him a little more than before. They listen to the words the man is speaking. He tells of the battle between Joseph and Alise, a vampire named Abraham, and a lost son called, Seth Wake. Sage also explains how the journal has been passed down generation to generation, awaiting the time Abraham would make his move. And the time is now. Lisa sits with her hands between her legs, off struck by this whole situation. As the conversation moves further along, she doesn't like what is being said. Sage removes a flask from the inside of his coat, takes a swig, and continues.

"It's in your blood Tommy. You are the only one who can stop Wake. The other two are simply half breeds. It's Wake that is the pure blood. He was born vampire, and more than that, he gained his mother's powers. They wont rest Tommy, not till they have what they want. All this death is due to one thing. And that's simply, somebody out there has what they need to keep Abraham alive. A very rare blood type that keeps a vampire young. Now don't get me wrong, they can live hundreds of year without it. But you see, Abraham's time is about to run out. We knew it would happen, the question was when. And the answer is now Tommy."

"I, I'm not sure I follow Sage. I mean, your telling me that someone in this city has some weird blood type that will keep these guys alive." Tommy shakes his head. He takes his right hand and rubs his eyes. "And what does it have to do with me, I'm a school kid. I can't stop these guys. This, I mean, this is crazy!"

Sage goes to speak, Lisa beats him to it. "No! Tommy isn't going any where near those guys. No way!"

"I understand your hesitation. But as I said, the blood is running through Tommy's blood. It's in him, he has the capability to stop this. I have Joseph Critton's slayer weapons Tommy. With them, not only will you have the proper weapons to kill them, but you will have your grandfathers spirit moving through you."

"Woo, wo, I have never killed anybody. I don't even know if I could if I had to. Even if these guys deserve it, I'm not sure it's in me to take another life. Sage, I'm just a high school student looking forward to going to the prom and making love to my girlfriend after. I'm not Joseph Critton, and I'm not a killer. And another thing, this isn't exactly"Buffy the vampire Slayer." This is real life!"

Sage stands, looks down at the pavement. He lights another cigarette. Then he turns back to Michael and Lisa. "Your absolutely right Tommy. This isn't Buffy, this is certainly not some Hollywood movie. This is the real thing. This is real life, just like you said. But what I am telling you is this. Cut and dry Tommy. If you ever want that sense of reality that you and your pretty little girlfriend had a month ago, if you ever want to make the prom..." Sage stops, he takes another drag off his cigarette, and takes a step closer to

Tommy, looks him straight in the eyes. "If you want your life back, and for the rest of your friends to live, you have to take them out. You have to Tommy, there's no one else. And should you choose to walk away from this, they will tear this city apart. They will kill all who get in their way until they find what it is they are looking for. And even upon finding it, the death may not stop, it could in fact be only the beginning. Oh, and one more thing Tommy, what if it's Lisa, what if Lisa is the one their looking for. So again, I say. Its up to you. Now lets get going, I will take you to the things you need to win this war!"

Tommy stands up, Lisa looks up in horror. "Tommy, what are you doing? You can't seriously be thinking of going after those monsters."

Tommy takes the cigarette from Sage's mouth, takes one drag and drops it on the ground, snuffing it out with his foot. "Lisa, I don't see where I have a choice. He's right, what if it is you. Now lets go, take me where we need to be."

Josie Lastings has settled down now. The hours in the day have passed, light has become darkness. The news of Dale Sanders and Toni Haley has really struck close to the heart of the family. And the worst of it, Michael has not returned. His phone only rings and rings. Steven Mass and Matthew Turry have joined them. All are mentally a mess. Jennifer has fixed Salisbury steak and mashed potatoes for dinner. The house is silent, the grown ups sit at the table staring at the food set before them. The only sound comes from Brad Lastings, sitting at his own little table. He is shaping his mashed potatoes into funny looking men. Then he makes an airplane sound with each bite of food he takes. In the living room, the phone rings. Derek excuses himself to answer it. It's James Smilot for Josie. Derek hands her the phone. "Hello?"

"Hey Josie, um, it James. My brother told me Michael didn't make work cause you had run into some trouble the other night. I was worried about you, so I, well, I thought I would call and check on you."

"Hi James. I'm ok, just a little shaken up. I'm a little sore all over more than anywhere else, but I'm gonna make it. I only hope I never sleep again." Josie tries to squeeze out a giggle, it's very minute.

James is silent a moment, of course, he was always this way on the phone. "That's good, um, I'm sorry! What I was saying is, its good your gonna make it. I'm sorry about the whole sleeping thing. You must have some awful nightmares. Um, I thought when you were feeling a little better, um, maybe I could take you out. You know, just to up your spirits a bit. We don't have to, I just, I thought maybe it would if we, ah, well, if we...

Josie cuts him short. "It sounds good James. You know, you really need to ease up a bit. Anyways, I heard about Dale, him and your brother were kind of close, is he holding up ok?"

James again pauses before replying. "Um, yeah. I guess he is holding up all right. He just, he just has a bit of an attitude. I think he is taking it harder than he shows. But, like I said, he is taking it pretty good."

"I hope so. James, I hate to run, but were eating dinner, and just got pretty bad news our self. My mom's best friend is gone too. She is taking it pretty bad. Anyway, I wish you and your family well. And I will call you tomorrow about going out. Alright, thanks. Bye, bye."

Josie hangs up the phone. Everyone looks at each other. Brad throws a spoon full of potatoes on the floor. It goes unnoticed. Steven Mass and Matthew Turry go back to eating. Derek does the same. Jennifer sits back in her chair, staring blankly at the food on her plate. She hasn't touched it. More tears stream down her face. Its not only the death of her best friend, or another one of her children missing. Its fear as well, paranoia, and the question repeating over and over in her head. Who's next? Who's next?

The night air has turned quite chilly. The wind has picked up a bit as a half moon shines in the star filled sky. Tommy Critton turns the air to warm and switches on the heater. They are almost to their destination. Sage directs him onto a dirt and gravel filled road. Dust swirls up around the car as he takes a sharp right onto the unpaved road. Lisa sits in the back seat, her head against the back dashboard. She had expected to see her best friend today. She had expected dinner out with Tommy, and maybe even a little messing around before going home. If someone had told her that morning she would be riding along with Tommy and some strange guy who had slipped up through the cracks of pavement heading for some unknown destination later that day, she would have told them they were crazy. But here she is. Going down some dark, deserted dirt road, with trees on either side, with a man that could very well be the anti-Christ. She thinks to herself of how crazy this whole ordeal seems. And along with all these thoughts swimming around in her head, she's scared. Up ahead, the road appears to stop in front of an old ramshackle barn. Or something like that. Whatever the hell it is, it seems the wind could blow it down at any moment.

The car stops a few feet away from the door of this weather beating, worn obstruction. Tommy takes a light from his glove box. He turns to Lisa. "You coming?"

Lisa looks at him as if he has two heads. "I wish! Of course I'm coming, you don't really think I'm gonna stay out here in the car all by myself do you. Out in the middle of nowhere, where I can hardly see my hand in front of my face. Are you nuts?"

Tommy opens his car door, Sage does the same. "A simple yes would have been fine darling." Tommy laughs. Lisa doesn't see the humor in it. She follows close behind her boyfriend just the same though. Sage leads them inside the old barn, he reaches out in the darkness for something. It's a lamp, an old hurricane lamp. He lights the wick, the flame illuminates the small area inside. On the right side is what looks to be old tackle, an antique lawnmower, and a Swinn bicycle. To the left and rear of the small building is nothing but bails of hay. Sage walks almost to the back wall and stops. Tommy follows, with Lisa right on his shirttail. Sage begins to move a stack of the hay bails from the wall to the little bit of walk way left between him and the rear wall. Underneath is more hay, spread across the cold ground under there feet. Or so it seems. Sage bends down, sweeps the hay off of an iron hatch, and lifts it open. The hinges squeal as he does so. Now Tommy and Lisa see what truly lies beneath. It's an iron chest placed in the ground. The man who only a few hours ago was a stranger, removes a long black bag from the chest. The bag is old but looks to still be in rather descent shape.

Lisa screams, "A spider, ooh, ooh. Get it Tommy, ohhh, get it!" Tommy rolls his eyes and laughs. He brushes the eight-legged insect from his girlfriend's leg then crushes it with his foot. Sage smiles.

"Don't worry young lady, your dear boy has got it all under control. Ok, now, lets get, shall we?"

"Gladly," Lisa calls, "I could have done without coming out here out all." She holds on to Tommy's arm as they walk back to the car. They put the bag in the trunk, and head back for the main road. The car comes to a stop at the start of the main road. Tommy looks for oncoming vehicles and prepares to move ahead. Sage opens his door and steps out.

"That's the end of the line for me my boy. You're on your own from here. But don't worry, when you take those weapons in you hand, all will be clear."

"What? There's nothing for miles. Where do you think you going. Come on, get back in the car. I need you" Tommy's voice sounds desperate, confused. Sage lights another cigarette, steps back and closes the car door.

"Don't worry about me young Critton. I will be just fine... and so will you. Now go on, get out of here. And remember, Joseph is with you, you're not alone."

"Sage!" Tommy calls to the stranger again as he turns to walk away. "I don't understand. How will I know what to do? And, where will you go? Who are you really? Come on man, get back in the car!"

Sage does not turn around, only keeps walking, he does answer though. "Can't do that Tommy. And trust me you'll know." Now he stops, and turns back, facing the car. "A friend Tommy Critton, a friend." A moment later, he turns back around and disappears into the darkness. Tommy stares for a moment, then turns to Lisa, mouth gaping. She stares back at him and pleads.

"Lets go Tommy, let's get the hell out of here, and back to civilization!" Tommy says nothing in return, only faces forward again and pulls back onto the road. Lisa slides into the front seat. She lays her head on his shoulder. And the two head back to town.

A bit off the road almost in the trees, a trailer sits in the moonlight. It looks condemned, dingy and dirty. Inside, Barry Spencer is still awake. The time is four AM. A hundred thoughts go through his head. Kevin Riley and Larry Stant were his best friends, and now they are gone. Taking from him by the icy grip of death. His mother is out with yet another man, it seems she is with someone different every week. Barry isn't sure she even knows he exists anymore. Sure she fixed him a plate for dinner before she went to stay the night with her new fling. It's sitting over by the television with flies hovering over it. But where is she now, when he really needs her? Off fucking some nobody that would never amount to anything. And maybe that's his own fate. He really doesn't know anymore. Things used to be so clear. He and his buddies were feared by the other students, Barry enjoyed that part. Now, he's not sure it was that great at all. Now, he has nobody to pal around with, no one to be cool with. The Barry Spencer that everyone knows is gone, and only a shell of a man remains. It doesn't have to be this way though, no he could change it. He could get a little revenge for his pals and earn the respect of many. Yes, that's it. Barry watches a roach crawl up the trailer wall and shudders. He has to get out of this shit hole. He jumps to his feet and jogs into the living room. His dad's old gun case sits between the living room and the kitchen. It's locked. No matter though, Barry breaks the glass with his elbow. Warm blood runs down his arm. He grabs a shotgun and a revolver from within. And walks out the door. Those motherfuckers would pay for messing with him and killing his friends. Yes, they would pay dearly! Barry Spencer walks with purpose across the plot of land in which his run down home rests. The shotgun rests on his shoulder, the revolver tucked under his belt, just inside his jeans. He speaks to the night. "Alright you son of a bitch, your day has come, your day of reckoning!"

A couple miles away, three dark figures stand in the shadows across the street from the Lastings house. The dampness of the night remains in the air but daybreak will soon be on the horizon. The three stand motionless, quiet, just as the Lastings house rests atop the hill before them. Seth Wake waits patiently for their time to come. They would make their move soon, make an entrance, and take what is needed. Seth speaks softly to his brothers, calmly. "Here we are boys, right there in that house you feast your eyes on right now. All we have to do is go in and get it. She stays alive, don't forget that. Abraham needs her alive. He grows weaker by the second. But no worry, it will all be over in the matter of a few hours. Only kill if you must to get to Josie, but we will get Josie, no matter what the cost." Again, all is silent, the three dark figures step forward. Even the wind calms, all is still!

Chapter 25

THE SUN BRINGS LIGHT to the sky as another day begins. The clock in Derek Lastings bedroom comes to life as the time turns to six-thirty. He slaps at the snooze button until it falls silent again. In the living room, Steven Mass stirs. He and Matthew stayed the night, gladly accepting Jennifer's invitation to do so. Josie Lastings is sound asleep in her own bed, and Brad tucked in warmly between his mother and father. The alarm does not even phase the boy. Derek lies in bed, eyes open, not wanting to get up and face the day. He knows he has to though. He had already missed one day of work, he hates missing work. It was for a good cause though. Today on the other hand, he knows his daughter is safe. His boy has him a little worried, but Michael has a life of his own and Derek understands this. He's sure the boy will call this afternoon or stop by or something. Derek sits up in bed, leans over, kisses his wife and little boy, and then swings his legs over the side of the bed.

The phone rings from the other room. Speak of the devil, Derek thinks to himself, and gets to his feet to go answer. In the living room, Steven Mass sits up quickly. He rushes to the phone, still half asleep. Otherwise he would never answer another resident's call. "Hello!"

"Steven, Steven is that you. Listen, its Tommy. Thank God your there. Is Matthew there with you?"

Steven rubs his eyes and yawns, "Yeah, yeah he here. Mrs. Lastings said we could..."

"Good, now listen. You have to get everybody up. Wake them up and have everyone stay together. You have to do it now." Tommy's words come quick and frantic.

Steven is slow to reply, "What? I'm not gonna wake the house up. What's going on?"

"Damn it Steve, just do it. And do it now, I'm on my way over. Your all in danger, you have to wake everyone. Get them all in the same room with one another!"

Steven is tired, Tommy's voice seems miles away. He becomes frustrated. "What the hell Tommy, its like six in morning. You want me, as a guest to..."

"Just do it Steven Mass, God Damn it just do it. I'll be there in ten minutes." The phone clicks.

"Hello? Hello?," no one answers, all Steven gets is a dial tone. Then, as if the windows were wired to the phone on impact, they shatter as Steve hangs the phone up. A white and a gray wolf lands almost on Matthew Turry's head. He wakes up with a scream, as he looks up he is staring right in the face of a nasty snarl. Something warm runs down his leg. Matt jumps back, Steven looks on with utter shock and amazement. Suddenly the front door implodes. Splinters of wood spray across the room. Seth Wake stands in the doorway. Throughout the house, all are jerked out of sleep from the sounds in the living room. Derek arrives just in time to watch two wolves take human forms. He hears his wife call to him from the bedroom. Derek takes a step back.

"Stay in the bedroom Jennifer, keep Brad with you in the bedroom and stay there. You hear me damn it, stay there!" Derek's voice booms throughout the house. Jennifer grabs Brad and retreats to the back of the bedroom. Derek grabs one of the dining room chairs behind him. Matthew sits completely still slumped against the front of the couch. Steven Mass grabs the glass lamp off the living room table and makes the first move. He swings the lamp over his head at the man in the doorway. Seth raises his arm in time for it to shatter over his forearm. Steven plows into Seth Wake shoulder first and both crash to the floor. Ash goes after them. Derek moves to stop him, Ambrose gets in the way. He swings the chair full force, catching Ambrose across the face and top of the head. The chair splinters and breaks in half. Ambrose goes to one knee, then shoots back up, grabbing Derek by the throat and thrusting him across the room. He lands hard against the fireplace.

Seth and Steven fall through the doorway and onto the porch. Steven punches his opponent once before he is grabbed from behind by Ash. Sharp fingernails dig into the young mans shoulders. Ash lifts Steve back to his feet then sends him crashing down the front steps. Finally, inside, Matthew Turry gets to his feet. He holds one of the legs from the broken chair in his hand. Ambrose rushes him, Matthew takes the sharp end of the broken wood and thrusts it into the gut of his attacker. They fall on top of one another. Ambrose wraps his hands around Matt's throat and prepares to choke the life out of him. A few feet behind them, Josie Lastings looks on in disbelief. Her father writhing in pain on the other side of the room. The struggle going on in the middle of the living room. It turns to horror as Seth steps back in the house, followed by Ash. Seth looks right at her, and takes chase. Josie runs for the back of the house. Meanwhile, Derek Lastings pulls himself back up, he grabs the metal fire-poking rod from beside the fireplace. Matthew Turry is in trouble. Derek has to act fast. He takes the point of his new weapon and brings it down as hard as he can into the back of Ambrose. He screams in pain and falls limp to the floor. Ash stalks toward Derek, just as he starts to walk passed the hole in the wall that is what's left of the front door, he is caught off guard.

Barry Spencer busts in, he shoves the barrel of his shotgun to Ash's chest. Their eyes meet, Barry pulls the trigger. Blood, guts and pieces of flesh explode out the back of Ash's body. His eyes become glazed as he collapses. "Not exactly the one I'm looking for, but fuck it."

Derek goes to one knee. He pushes Ambrose off of Matthew and helps him up. He motions to Barry and calls to him to go check on Steven outside. Just then, Steve stumbles in the front door, and falls. From the other room, Josie screams. Derek takes off in a sprint for the back of the house. Barry Spencer follows. Matt goes over to Steven Mass. He is conscious, but the spill down the concrete steps did some damage. Behind him, Ambrose slowly rises again. He reaches back and pulls the rod out of his back. Matthew turns around just in time to be stabbed right through his shoulder. Ambrose grabs his hair and sinks his teeth into the neck of his wounded prey. Steven tries to pull himself up, no good. Somethings broken, it feels as if his whole body is broken.

Josie slides down the back wall of the washroom as Seth's shadow falls over her. He reaches down and grabs her shirt, pulls her to her feet. She screams and starts pounding his chest with her hands. Seth forcefully slams her back against the wall. Her head takes quite a blow, and renders her unconscious. Seth lets her slide back down into the floor. Footsteps pound the floor behind him. He turns to face them. Derek comes full force, striking Seth in the face with a hard right hand. He stumbles back, Derek pulls back for another swing. Seth Wake wave his hand, an unseen force sends his attacker flailing backwards, right into the oncoming Barry Spencer. Both land on kitchen floor with a thud. Barry is the first back to his feet. Seth recognizes the boy from their last struggle, and understands the boy knows him as well. Barry raises the shotgun and fires. Buckshot fills the back washroom, sure to hit everything within. Seth's eyes go black, the bullets are all pulled to him, and not a one makes it to Josie behind him. The blast hits Seth and sends him crashing into a shelf behind him. Barry looks to fire again, this time he thinks better of it and tosses the gun aside. He pulls the revolver from his jeans and takes a few steps into the washroom. He fires again on the man that killed his friends. Seth takes another bullet, this one in the shoulder. His pain is tremendous, but he still manages to fight back. Seth claps his hand together, his eyes black as night. The hot water heater in the corner rips out of its place and is slung across the room. It slams into an unsuspecting Barry Spencer, as he falls the water heater lands on top of him and rolls off to the side. Derek Lastings goes for the gun in Barry's hand. Seth struggles to walk, he stumbles his way to Derek Lastings. Derek raises the gun.

Ambrose lets Matthew Turry's body fall to the floor. Steven grabs his leg in an attempt to keep him from the others. Ambrose grabs him by the hair and lifts him. He takes the knife from his side, ready to gut Steven Mass like a fish.

"Hey asshole, you want to kill somebody. Kill me!" A voice calls to Ambrose from outside, he turns to find Tommy Critton standing only a couple yards to his left. He shoves the knife into Steve's gut and drops him. Tommy wields a silver sword in his hand, there's also two or three other weapons strapped around his waist. Ambrose steps onto the front porch. The two of them stare at each other, like two gun fighters in the old west, ready to draw their guns and fire on the other. Tommy grasps the sword with both hands and swings, Ambrose jumps back just in time to dodge the attack. In a flash he comes back at Tommy, he backhands him, causing the want to be hero back on his heels. Ambrose lets his nails grow to about four inches and slashes his opponent across the chest. Tommy brings the sword back around, this time slicing the vampires arm wide open. Steam seeps from the wound, and the nocturnal beast howls in pain. Ambrose throws himself backward, as he hits the porch floor he changes back to the gray wolf that crashed through the front window. Tommy holds his ground, the animal leaps. He tries to bring the sword around to catch it, not fast enough. The wolf pounces on him, he lands hard on his back. Sharp teeth tear into Tommy's shoulder. He reaches for his belt, and removes a flask. He struggles to get the top off as the wolf gnaws on his left shoulder. The wolf shrinks back a moment to move in for the kill. Tommy watches as those sharp teeth go for his neck. The top of the flask falls away, Tommy Critton douses the animals head with the contents inside. The gray wolf cries out in pain as the very hair on its head burns, more steam seeps up into the air. It retreats momentarily, taking its paws and trying to rub the liquid off its head. Tommy doesn't hesitate. He grabs another weapon from his belt, this one looks like a miniature sickle. He drives it deep into the side of the creature's body. Again Ambrose begins to change, the wolf shrinks away and a bat tries to flutter away. It's wounded and slow. Tommy reaches for the last little toy in his arsenal. The gun feels small in is hand, but never the less he reacts quickly. The weapon fires a webbing of sort into the air. It wraps the black flying creature into a tiny ball. It falls to the porch. The animal screeches. The noise is almost deafening. Black smoke pours off the little body of the thing that was Ambrose. All that's left when the smoke is gone is the skeleton of a small flying animal. Tommy lifts his sword from the spot it fell. He looks at his shoulder, its pretty bad. No time for that now, he had to keep going, the worst is still to come. Tommy enters the house, he helps Steven to the couch, removes the knife and has Mass apply pressure to the wound. "Hang in there Stevie, hang in there."

Movement catches Tommy's eye. Ash struggles to get to his feet. The hole in his chest and back remains, the animal is wounded, but not dead. Tommy braces the silver sword in his hands and walks over to whats left of Ash. The vampire gets to its knees just in time for the sword to slice into its neck. Ash's eyes bulge as the blade cuts clean through. His head rolls of his shoulders. More black smoke spews into the air from the neck of the dying creature.

Seth grabs the gun as it fires, the bullet takes his left ear. He screams in pain and at the same time becomes enraged. He wrestles the gun away from Derek Lastings and forces the man to the floor. Seth pulls his knife out and attempts to stick it into Derek's chest. The man grabs his attackers wrist hoping he is strong enough to keep the razor sharp blade away from his body. Seth Wake looks deep into Derek Lastings eyes. Suddenly, Derek feels himself pull his arms away involuntarily. They go to his side, Seth raised the knife into the air and brings it down. Only he doesn't go for the chest. He stabs the man deep into his side. Derek hollers in pain. Seth grabs his shoulders, leans over and buries his teeth into Daddy Lastings neck, and he feeds. From the bedroom, Derek can hear his son Brad screaming, "I want daddy, I want my daddy." Jennifer keeps her arms wrapped tightly around the boy. They remain huddled in a corner. Jennifer weeping, and Brad screaming for daddy.

Seth raises his head, he's had his fill. Still a pain rips through him, and he realizes Ambrose is gone, and Ash is in need of blood. Seth returns to his feet, he looks back at Josie and starts for the front of the house. He stops, and turns back for the girl. He steps over Derek and Barry and goes for Josie. Seth Wake lifts the young girl over his shoulder and again turns back for the living room. As he steps back over Derek Lastings, he falls to one knee. The pain of his other brother's death shoots through him. How, how could they both be dead. What the hell went wrong. Seth tries to concentrate on his father, the only one he now has left in the world. Seth again starts for the living room. Here he finds Ash's dead smoking body, and Tommy Critton standing over him. Their eyes meet. Seth drops Josie. "So Tommy Critton, your the one killing off my family. Why don't you try me? And don't worry, this time, Wake against Critton, only one will die. You can't beat me Tommy, you're not strong enough!"

Seth thrusts his right hand in Tommy's direction, as if he is throwing something at him. Tommy leaves his feet, soars into the fish tank behind him and crashes through it. Water, fish, glass and gravel go everywhere. Seth Wake moves forward, his eyes are glazed, black and cold. He lifts his hand again, palm up, and thrusts it to the left. Tommy Critton is once again slung through the air. This time he plunges into the china cabinet on the other side of the room. He crashes thought the glass, crushing the face of the once beautiful piece of furniture. His battered body falls to the floor. The china hutch teeters then falls forward on top of him.

Seth smirks. "Nice doing business with you Tommy, but I can't stay. Ms. Lastings and I have a hot date. Sorry you wont be able to join us." Seth once again goes for Josie. She is half way to her feet when she sees Seth coming her way. She screams and stumbles her way into her mother's bedroom. Josie slams the door and locks it behind her. Jennifer calls to her.

"Josie, oh God baby, what the hell is going on out there. Are you ok, where's Derek?"

"I don't know, oh I don't know mom," Josie feels the tears rolling down her cheek. "Get back mom, get back."

Josie and Jennifer, Brad still in her arms, move to the very back of the room. The bedroom door flies open, ripping form the hinges and landing on the other side of the room. Seth walks in and comes straight at Josie. Jennifer puts Brad down and charges him. "MOM NO." Josie screams.

Too late. Seth backhands her, she crashes to the floor, hurt and crying. Brad runs to his mom, Josie catches the tail end of his shirt but loses him. Seth grabs the boy and lifts him into the air. Brad screams and kicks his legs. Josie watches in horror, she just knows she's about to watch her baby brother get torn apart. He's just a baby. To her surprise, Seth Wake sets the boy down gently next to his mother. Brad wraps his arms Jennifer's neck. Josie backs herself into the corner. Seth closes in, he grabs her hair and kisses her deeply on the lips. A second later, all the room goes dark, and again Josie loses consciousness.

Seth kneels and touches Ash on the shoulder on his way out, gives Tommy one last glance, and exits the house. Here he finds Ambrose, or what is left of him. A tear runs down Seth's face as he sets Josie down again. He rips the netting off the skeleton of this form of his brother. Seth touches the head of the bat, it returns to its human form. The sight isn't pretty. The body is ravaged. Strands of meat and skin cling to the bones, the eyes in the skull are sunk in. And the veins remain in tact running through out the skeleton. Seth lowers his head. "Adi soi tila mina, pela ri yew unae." He returns to his feet and looks to the sky, "My dear Ash and Ambrose."

Seth lifts Josie up one more time, sirens fill the air. They are close, very close. Two tear up the street and come to a screeching holt in front of the house. Wakes had enough, he doesn't have time for this. He takes his free hand and clinches it tight. The cop car on the left explodes, the officers exiting the vehicle go with it. Seth releases his fist and clenches it again. The second car turns to a giant fireball, so much for the authorities. He realizes more will be soon to follow. But they will be too late. He closes his eyes, now holding Josie with both arms. His look begins to change, only this time he does not grow any smaller. Suddenly something slices into Seth's back. The formation stops, Wake returns to his normal self. He goes to his knees as the intense burning continues to curse his back. Seth lets Josie come to rest on the ground. He reaches back and pulls the object from within. Tommy Critton calls to him from behind.

"Don't hunt what you cant kill Wake. Now lets finish this, its me or you. How does that go, oh yes, There can be only one you fucking son of a bitch!"

Seth turns around, he drops the miniature sickle to the sidewalk. Tommy slowly makes his way down the first set of steps. "No powers this time, just you and me. My sword against your brute strength. And those ugly ass fangs of yours." Seth's eyes return to normal as his steps bring him ever closer to Tommy.

"Well that hardly seems fair Tommy. I mean, you're at such a disadvantage. And aside from all that, I don't have time to play your game." Seth grabs his knife and slings it for Tommy. He knocks it away with his own weapon, and makes his attack. The sword cuts through the air only inches from Seth's body. Wake spins and kicks Critton in the chest. He falls backward, his head almost smacking the concrete. Seth stalks over him, Tommy kicks his legs out from under him and leaps back to his feet. He picks up the sword at his feet. Seth also returns to a standing position. He attacks, Tommy manages to slice his opponents shoulder in the rush, but nothing more. Seth grasps both Tommy's arms with his hands. Both men wrestle for the sword, they spill to the ground. The weapon comes loose from Critton's hand. Seth leans in, he is going for the neck. Tommy struggles to free one of his hands and does so. He grabs a handful of dirt and lets it fly, right in the face of Seth Wake. Now he shoves him off, and lunges for the sword. His hand grasps it and just in time. One of the large concrete flowerpots are hurling at him. Tommy shatters it with one slice of the sword, and in the same motion brings the sword back around and into Seth's stomach. The vampire writhes in pain but does not make a sound. His eyes open, they are blood red and very animal like. Suddenly Tommy feels his throat begin to close up on him. Soon, no air can enter or leave his lungs. He's choking, Tommy brings his hands to his throat, only what really can he do. He drops to his knees, his sword is still stuck in Wakes gut. The world around him starts to spin, and it gets darker and darker.

The knife in your boot Tommy, use the knife in your boot

Tommy reaches back to his ankle, lifts the pant leg and finds a knife. His last chance of survival. With all he has left, Tommy pulls the knife and lets it fly. It finds its mark and it punctures Seth Wake's neck and sinks in. Seth stumbles, then falls to the ground. Tommy's airwaves reopen, he gasps to regain his breath. He collapses as well, spent and out of breath. Seth Wake fumbles to get hold of the knife in his throat, his whole body feels on fire. And he realizes he's dying. His hand falls away from the knife. His flesh begins to turn an ashy gray.

A shadow falls over Seth's dying body. His eyes take in the view of his fathers form standing above him. "Fa...ther, no..." The knife is pulled from Seth's neck and tossed away, the sword follows. The form that is Abraham falters then returns. He kneels down and kisses his son on the forehead. Then it's gone.

Seth can feel life begin to reenter his body. He is deathly weak, but alive. More sirens in the distance fall upon his ears. Its over, Seth knows it is. He struggles to reach his feet. His skin still burns slightly, and still holds it's ashy gray color. The sirens get closer. Tommy Critton sits up. Seth closes his eyes, his fathers life source is fading, he used the last of his strength to save his own. No, it not over, it's not over. Seth leaps on top of Tommy, his fangs sink into the hero's neck, and he begins to feed. Begins to take the very substance that will completely regenerate him. As he drinks from Tommy's blood, Tommy feels himself begin to weaken. He grabs Seth by the hair, tries to force him off, it no use. He starts to realize, he may never hold Lisa again. May never see another sunrise or another nightfall. Then...

It stops.

Seth pulls away and looks to the sky. "No, No. FATHER! FATHER!" The pain hits Seth Wake like a train. He doubles over and lands beside Tommy. He is too late, Abraham is dead. "No! No! No, no, no!"

Tommy recognizes his opportunity. He fights to get to his hands and knees, crawls over to the nearest weapon. Tommy grabs the dagger and pulls himself to his feet. He walks over to Seth, he looks down at the tears rolling down his face. He whispers father time and again. Tommy drops to his knees, lifts the knife above his head with both hands, and brings it down. He plants it right in the small of the back of Seth's body. Then he lets himself return to the ground. He watches as the black smoke rises into the air, and then...

Tommy knows Seth is gone. A black shape flapping in the wind. Then there is nothing. Only the sounds of sirens. Several Police vehicles arrive on the scene. City cops, state cops, even a few Federal. Moments later, two ambulances arrive and the site becomes very hectic very fast. Tommy watches as the EMT's rush back and forth, the firemen, the cops. He watches as he is loaded into the back of one of the ambulances. And he wonders, "Is there anyone else? Is there anyone else left alive?"

Chapter 26

Two years later...

THE SUN HAS PEAKED in the sky, it beams down over land bringing temperatures to the mid-nineties. It's the last day of June in the city of Spontania. Josie Lastings, her mother Jennifer, and little Brad left Trench a couple months after losing Derek and Michael. The journey had been rough, getting from there to here. But they had done it. The new home has two floors, four bedrooms and two baths. The fourth bedroom dedicated to Derek and Michael Lastings. Favorite photographs, a few of the precious belongings and fresh flowers every week. The Lastings surroundings are quite different than what they had been. It's more of a suburban life now. Lots of houses close together. In the back yard, they have an in ground swimming pool. The family spends most of the hot days here, by or in the water.

Josie relaxes in a lawn chair, watching the guys show off their best dives from the board. Her mom had decided a few weeks before to throw this party. All their friends from Trench were invited. Most of them have shown up already. Tommy and Lisa relax together in hot tub across the yard. Josie's boyfriend, James Smilot is showing off with the rest of the guys. His brother Timothy, Steven Mass, and Kenny Marks. And even Barry Spencer had shown up, him and the gang have become close over the past two years. A lot had happened in that time. Josie and Craig Johnson gave it a go, until finally she realized it for what it really was. Just a high school crush. She's happy with James though, they make a great pair.

Jennifer welcomes Sandra and Eric Mays as they walk through the side gate. Tommy's sister Tara arrives a few minutes later. Yep, the gang is all here. Josie Lastings smiles as she looks around at her friends and family. They had taking a walk through the depths of hell, but it's behind them now. The memories of the loved ones lost will always remain, and sometimes even hurt. Josie though, for the most part is passed the whole terrible ordeal. Life as she knew it back then would never be the same. She accepted that over time, and together with everyone helping each other, they have started a new life. A happy life. Josie Lastings takes a sip of iced tea, lays back and closes her eyes. And lets the warm sun wash over her. She feels relaxed, at peace. Everything is going to be just fine, she thinks to herself, just fine!

Authors Note

THERE ARE SO MANY people I would like to thank, for encouragement and standing behind me. The truth is, I never could have finished this book without them. First I would like to thank my mother and father for all they have done for me. My dad is no longer with us, so I dedicated this piece of work to him. Moving along, I have to tell my brother Matthew how much I truly appreciate him standing behind me for all these years. If not for him, none of this would have been possible. You truly stuck by me through my struggles in writing, and for that, I thank you. But I can't give him all the credit, many wonderful people have touched my life. All my family and friends have been great. Bobby, you made this all possible, thanks man. And most importantly, I want to thank my two daughters, Josie and Sadie for giving me an ongoing reason to move forward. I love you both! You are with out a doubt the fire within that keeps me going. The wind beneath my wings. Last but not least, I want to thank you, the reader for reading what it is that I write. And I want to thank God for giving me the ability to write what it is that you read. On a special note, rest well baby Hannah, with all our love!

www.ingramcontent.com/pod-product-compliance
Lightning Source LLC
Chambersburg PA
CBHW050743250626
47155CB00005B/1893